LESBIAN LUST

LESBIAN LUST

EROTIC STORIES

EDITED BY

SACCHI GREEN

CLEIS
PRESS

Published in the United States by Cleis Press, Inc., 2246 Sixth Street, Berkeley, California 94710.

Printed in the United States.
Cover design: Scott Idleman
Cover photograph: Barnaby Hall/Getty Images
Text design: Frank Wiedemann
Cleis logo art: Juana Alicia
First Edition.
10 9 8 7 6 5 4 3 2 1

ISBN: 978-1-57344-403-3

Contents

| INTRODUCTION

L ust: it's the engine that drives us wild on the way to getting us off, and lesbian lust is the heart, soul and red-hot core of this anthology. Within this shared journey each of these eighteen writers takes us for a vividly different ride on the way to intense, fulfilling lesbian sex. In some of the stories, we claim our right to lightning-strike, no-strings, purely physical sex; in some, the emotional complexity and depth stir us as profoundly as the physicality; in some, erotic fantasies are played out in ways that tease the mind as well as the body and a few defy any description or classification except that of superheated originality.

For me, the pleasure of reading and selecting these stories has been close to lust itself. Familiar, well-known voices whose very names bring on a tingle have outdone themselves, and newer writers with unexpected styles and perspectives have given me an erotic jolt of lust at first sight. There are stories here that push a wide range of buttons in just the way I like them pushed, along with innovative work that comes close to nudging even my own boundaries to the limit. Variety is also the spice of lust.

Within all that variety, there are some groups of stories with similar themes but different presentations: sex and cars, for example. Fran Walker's "A Midwinter Night's Dream" is both surreal and gritty; Crystal Barela's "Camshaft Cutie" is desert hot and humorous and C. B. Potts's "The Angel Connection" takes age and power differentials and turns them upside down in an all-girl repair shop. Taking the car motif in another direction, Ren Peters involves two longtime lovers in a threesome with a classic Porsche Boxster under a "Lovers' Moon.

Established couples are also at the center of DeJay's "Never Too Old," blending humor with true intimacy in a Province-town sex toy store setting and Cheyenne Blue's "A Story about Sarah," an atmospheric, poetic account of interracial lovers in the Australian Outback. In a very different vein, the partner of Catherine Lundoff's protagonist in "Reunion at St. Mary's" arranges to fulfill her schoolgirl fantasy with the former members of the girls' hockey team. Other couples who know each other well but are still working out the nature of their relationships— with the help of plenty of sex—appear in Delilah Devlin's "The Weekend" and Jade Melisande's "Are You Gonna Be My Girl." In my own contribution, "Danger," another couple's chance encounter at a turning point in history brings back traumatic memories of their first meeting in the chaos of war.

Youth and maturity strike sparks in Sommer Marsden's smooth and sassy "The Girl with the Bettie Page Bangs" and Jove Belle's "Love and Devotion," with its Southern-noir atmosphere. The lush tropical settings of Rachel Kramer Bussel's "Swollen" and Andrea Dale's "Lost and Found" enhance the sensuality of their encounters, while Teresa Noelle Roberts's "Not Afraid to Get Her hands Dirty" is no less sexy for being literally down-to-earth, and R. G. Emanuelle's "The Office Grind" shows more action going on under the desk than above it.

Two of the most gripping stories push the edge in very different ways. In "August Crazies," Miel Rose shows the BDSM world of power exchange with scorching detail, while illuminating the underlying complexities and vulnerabilities with tenderness and no less heat. Kenzie Mayer's "Canvas" paints a darker picture, where sexual drive blends with artistic obsession until they become indistinguishable.

I'm asked sometimes to name favorite stories from the books I edit, but isn't that like choosing between chocolate and champagne or apples and pomegranates? Lust comes in many flavors, all of them intense. In these eighteen stories you'll find sweet sex, bittersweet sex, salty and sweaty sex, creamy-smooth sex and sex with crunch to it. Go ahead, take a bite and then another and another; I hope you'll savor them all as much as I do.

Sacchi Green
Amherst, Massachusetts

THE GIRL WITH THE BETTIE PAGE BANGS

Sommer Marsden

'm not really a dirty old broad. Truly. If it hadn't been for my brand-spanking-new, thousand-dollar rock, I never would have met Callie. Ever. But I had bought a very expensive new computer that kept fucking everything up. And by everything, I mean *everything:* PDFs, spreadsheets, hell, even the Internet. And every time it did so, I had to grab my flash drive and run to the library. When you work for yourself you have to make do.

So here I am, sweating my ass off in my car because the air is broken. I pull up to the library (I had been there the day before) and there she sits, outside on her break, smoking a cigarette and picking lazily at a string on her skinny black jeans.

I am not a dirty old broad, I swear.

But damn: she's long and lean, hair as dark as a crow's wings, with a painted doll face and red, red lips. She sports a small black cardigan and what gets me—Bettie Page bangs.

I avert my eyes and grab my bag and go right by her. She's maybe nineteen or twenty to my thirty-seven. No way, José. It's a momentary flash of attraction and extreme insanity. It will pass. But I can't keep my eyes from darting for a fast peripheral check: small, teacup-sized breasts; tiny waist; long, coltish legs; big blue eyes and lashes that make me want to beg or swear, maybe both.

"Hiya," she says and smiles. I fear my knees may buckle.

I nod. "Nice day." I push my feet forward toward the side entrance and then she stuns me.

"You're back."

Fuck.

"Yes. Yes, I am. I bought a very expensive paperweight, it seems." My face colors and my hand touches the door handle, but I don't want to go in. The girl with the Bettie Page bangs is talking to me. Me!

"I'm sorry. The regulars usually have a reason. Research paper, book; mental disability, so they come to watch Superman videos over and over and over again. 'Cause you know he's going to save the world, Supe is." She winks when she says it, but there is no cruelty in her voice, only good humor and a touch of sadness. Oddly enough, I know exactly which person she is referring to.

"Mine is, I work from home and I bought a brand-new computer that won't let me do certain things."

Somehow, the girl with the Bettie Page bangs and I are now climbing the stairs to the computer center together. How did that happen? I usually do not go gaga and soft headed over women, no matter how pretty.

"Like what?" She twirls a poker-straight length of hair around her finger and pops her gum, something that would be a major offense coming from anyone else in the world but somehow when she does it, it's sexy.

"Cut and paste."

She blinks at me, shocked. "No shit?" Her eyes dart around.

She's at work, probably the wrong word choice. But I laugh out loud and nod.

"No shit."

"I'll put you on number thirteen," she says and smiles. "I'm Callie, B-T-W."

"B-T-W?"

"By the way."

I feel the blush rise. "Right. Sorry. I'm Janie. D-A-B."

"D-A-B?"

"Dumb-ass blonde."

Her smile is wider than ever and perfect. "Thirteen for you, D-A-B."

"Oh, great. More bad luck," I tease.

"Actually, thirteen is my lucky number."

"Because that's how old you are?" I laugh and so does she. I'm fishing and we both know it.

"Actually, I'm twenty-two, thank you very much." She bats those long black lashes at me and my insides turn hot and liquid. I want her. Bad.

"I just meant—"

"Oh, don't worry. I know I look young. I figure it's a perk. When I'm fifty, I'll look like a smoking forty-year-old cougar, yeah?" She touches my hand when she says that, and my pussy responds as if she's licked me. I'm in deep, deep shit, my friend.

"Yeah, I'm sure you're gonna look smoking hot whatever the age." But I feel pretty good. My thirty-seven isn't so bad compared to twenty-two. I was thinking maybe nineteen and then I'd have to kill myself for being a dirty, dirty perv.

"Number thirteen, then. I'll make sure you get a few extra minutes. You know. To cut and paste."

I sit and realize my hands are shaking, hard. I try to focus on the report I had been doing at home. No go. All I can think of is the way her fingers felt running up my arm, her fingers still warm from the sun, my arm suddenly cooler from the air-conditioning. It's easy to picture her on her knees, pushing those perfect crisp bangs from her forehead; that pale pink tongue darting out to taste me. It would be so easy to cup the back of her head and guide her, show her exactly how I like it, how fast, how wet, how hard. I'd make her see just how I like to come and...

"Okay?" she says. *Shit*. She's right at my shoulder. When did she move? How quietly she must have moved. Have I really just made that squealy yelp I am so famous for in front of the other six people at the bank of computers?

Someone laughs.

I have.

"Fine. Fine, it's going just fine," I stammer.

She stares at my blank screen and flashing cursor and grins a knowing grin that makes my stomach flutter like soft wings on a hard breeze. "I can see that."

When she leaves, I suck in a deep rush of cool filtered air and let my heart stop flopping around like a fish. A small box pops up on the computer.

LIBRARY CONTENT: WANNA GO TO LUNCH?

For just a second, I have no fucking clue what that is. I think I have been hacked or there's a virus or possibly, I have started to hallucinate from all the stress. I shove my hands into my honey-dark hair that is desperately in need of a good cut from chin length to cheek length and then my eyes find her. She's at the desk, twirling that hair again, popping her gum, watching me, smiling at me. Her lips are candy-apple red and my cunt grips up around nothing at all.

God, yes, I want to go to lunch, if lunch is her in my bed

naked and fucking me. I shake my head and realize I have just said no. I look up and smile, nod. She grins back.

My small house is five minutes away. Five minutes that somehow, today, with Callie in the front seat next to me, feel like five or six hours, roughly. I push my foot to the floor and my ancient Jeep lurches forward. She puts her hand on my thigh. "Don't get us arrested. I get an hour break."

"Right. Sorry. What do you want to eat?"

She grins and my heart lurches along with the Jeep. "You, of course. I thought you understood that. I'm not seducing you, am I?"

"Yes."

She blinks those impossibly blue eyes, and I can smell the mint from her gum. Will it make my pussy tingle and cool me or will it burn? I am dying to know. "But I like it. Please don't stop."

She keeps her hand on my thigh and pushes it higher. "Don't worry. I never stop once I want something."

"Good to know." I practically take out my garbage can when I park out front. My nerves are high but the urge to get her naked and see her bare is worse. I grab her hand and pull her to my front door. My door is red. Whenever I see it I think of magic and happy endings. I hope this is one.

"I'm not going to run away. You don't have to drag me," she says, and her little finger does a soft sweep of my palm. My nipples go taut and my belly, too. My ears start to ring. I turn my key, push the door open, get her inside. I push her to the wall and kiss her because I think I might actually die if I don't get my lips on her somewhere.

I push her to the cream-colored wall and her little black sweater whispers. The pearl buttons put up a fight but I win, getting them undone one by slippery one. Her bra is black—big shock. Her breasts are pink, her nipples mauve. Her skin smells like gardenias and sunshine. She dips her head and a curtain of shiny dark hair falls over her nipple. She kisses me before I can kiss her breast.

Her fingers lace into my hair and she tugs hard enough for me to make a sound in my throat, hard enough for me to feel the tightening of my insides and the sharp beat of arousal in my pelvis. She tugs again and bites my lip. "I'd love to do it in the living room, but I want to see your bed. Where is your bed?"

I tug her some more and she's up the steps with me, but her sweater's still down on my hardwood floor.

We make a sharp left turn and tumble. We're going down and not that way yet, but it's fine because my bedroom is so small that three medium steps will connect you with the mattress and faded blue satin bedding. We hit, we bounce, we laugh. Her lips on me are like soft little petals. She sucks my nipples through my Oyster Bay T-shirt, leaving wet spots on the pale green fabric. My hands can't decide whether to tug at my jeans or her much darker, much skinnier jeans. Callie solves that. She yanks my buttons and pulls at hers and somehow in this tangle of clothes and her long hair, we're bare from the waist down. "I hope you don't think I'm a slut," she says and I freeze.

Then she tosses her head back and laughs so long and so loud that I can only laugh too. "No, I never thought—"

"I'm kidding. Mostly. And it's not like it would stop me anyhow," she says, kissing a wet trail over my shoulder. My whole body shivers even though my bedroom is a bit too warm and stagnant.

"I think you're stunning," I say a little too baldly for my taste. I don't like to tell the unadulterated truth too much when it comes to these things. It's usually sort of like baring my throat to a blade. But for some reason I tell her exactly how I feel.

"And I think you are the sexiest woman I have seen in…" She shuts her eyes like she's thinking. "Well, ever."

That makes me snort because it can't possibly be true. My brain forgets to tell her this because she's pushing long, slim pale fingers into my pussy and they're sinking in one at a time, effortlessly, like she's playing an instrument. Me.

I roll to top her, pushing her silken hair out of her face so I can see her beautiful eyes. She's so pretty she almost appears not real but some flesh-and-blood doll come to life to torture me with dirty thoughts.

"Kiss me. Don't just stare."

I kiss her and taste the strong mint and soda and cigarettes on her tongue. My hands wander the smooth, buttery valleys of her skin, find the small perfect swells of her tits, and my hips rise and fall with the tide of my want. I want her, more than I can ever recall wanting anyone in my life. I keep waiting to take a breath and find her gone.

Her fingers are in me to the top knuckle, kneading and exploring all the softest, warmest parts of me. I start to crest— closer and closer to my orgasm, and I might object except it will free me up to focus on her, and that is the best premise of all. She wiggles out of my embrace, bends like some rubber plaything, and in a heartbeat her mouth is on me and my pelvis is surging up to meet her tongue, my clit bathed in the perfect hot moisture of her mouth.

"Jesus. You should have—" I gasp. "I want to—"

"You'll get what you want. But first me. What I want." Her mouth works in tandem with her fingers. She's a sorceress, a magician. She makes me come in four swift licks and a thrust. I let it go; the warm purple wave of orgasm takes me under, and I let it. Because now I can have my way and she can't say boo.

She's long and lean but I work out a few hours a day most

days and flipping her over and around and up is as easy as making the bed. So I do. I push her back and slide my hands under her soft, small ass, and I pinch just enough that her eyes slam shut and her mouth forms a red little O. She sighs, and I know she likes the tiny sparkly bites of pain with her fucking. So there you go; I learned something new.

I put my mouth on her, push the ridge of my teeth to the pale skin of her mound and test. She arches up into the sharpness and I lick, pushing my teeth harder into her skin. She'll have a soldier line of purple marks there tomorrow on her waxed mound, above her pussy, above her clit, above the entrance to her body, where I've been. I like the thought of that mark on her.

Her little fists clutch at my faded bedsheets; her knees climb up and down to nowhere under my belly as I fuck her with my tongue. I keep her right on edge, the pretty girl with the Bettie Page bangs, Callie. I keep her right on edge until she is quite literally crying. I slip my fingers into her and she is so goddamn wet. I'd give a million dollars to make a visit to my closet for some toys, but the clock is a traitor and says we have twenty minutes. I make do, fucking her with my fingers and licking her right up to the sharp paper-cut edge of coming and then backing off.

When she starts sobbing, shuddering under me, her lips moving but making no sound, I let her go. I thrust hard, arch my fingers against the warm spongy parts of her. I suck her clit like a hard candy and my mouth fills with her sweetness and light.

We lie there, her heartbeat visible inside her thigh, mine thundering in my ears.

"Gosh. That was…"

"Amazing."

"Awesome."

"Perfect," I say, laughing.

"Just one thing." She's toeing my pussy and her knee is right in my face. I bite her lightly and she jumps, her big toe brushing my clit.

God, I want her, all over again. "Yeah?"

"Don't think I'm pushy or anything, but..."

"What?"

"Will you have dinner with me?"

I grin, nibble her knee again, the inside of one pale white thigh. I run my fingers over a dark brown mole on her flank. "What's on the menu?"

"Me."

"Count me in."

REUNION AT ST. MARY'S

Catherine Lundoff

Bridget Marie Riordan O'Halloran was depressed. It wasn't so much that work was insanely stressful, though that was part of it, or that Vic and all her friends seemed to have forgotten her birthday, though that didn't help. It was the clipping from the parish newspaper, courtesy of her mother, that put her over the edge. Sister Agnes Mercy Byrnes had been taken up to heaven, or so it said. But from what Bridget remembered of her, she was more likely to be torturing the Devil below than hovering on a cloud above.

Where she was didn't matter so much as the fact that she was gone. It was the passing of an era. Sister Agnes had been the terror, among other things, of Bridget's high school years. She'd spent many hours over the years masturbating over her memories of the spanking the nun had once given her in the principal's office. Imagining those firm hands on her young flesh gave her a thrill even now. She pictured Sister Agnes going even further and pulling down her white virginal panties and... Vic walked in a moment later to find her with her hand between her legs.

"Hi, sweetie. Ooh, that looks like fun. What triggered this?" Vic grabbed the little clipping as Bridget jerked her hand out of her pants. Vic gave her a look of pure disbelief. "You're jilling off to Sister Agnes's obituary?"

Bridget turned bright red and tried to come up with a good explanation. Then she gave up and went on the attack instead. "You forgot my birthday! Some girlfriend you are." She crossed her arms over her chest to hide the nipples poking through her shirt. Sister Agnes's hands had been pretty amazing in that last fantasy.

"I knew you were going to say that." Vic grinned triumphantly as she dropped onto the couch. She ran one hand down Bridget's thigh with a possessive pressure that never failed to make her pay attention. "I've got a little surprise for you, babe. Kind of appropriate too, given your new ghoulish hobby. We're going to your tenth high school reunion. My treat."

Bridget's jaw dropped. No way. Sister Julia and Father Williams would run them out of Sacred Heart Parish at the head of a torch-wielding mob. Vic just didn't understand how things worked at parochial school. But before she could say a word, Vic had her in a lip-lock that soon turned to other things. Once Vic was holding Bridget down and pounding her fist into her wet and desperate pussy, going home for the reunion sounded just fine. Besides, it was two months away; she had plenty of time to change Vic's mind.

But somehow, they never got around to talking about it. Every time she tried, Vic was too busy or was all over her so she gave up, resigning herself to the trip from hell. It would be even worse if they ended up staying with her parents. She just hoped her mother wouldn't say the rosary over them again when she thought they were sleeping.

Despite all her worries, she started to wonder if some of her old friends would be there. Monica had come out after graduation. That was inevitable. If James Dean had ever been reincarnated as a Catholic high school girl, Monica was it. Then there was Mary Eileen. She'd never forget that one slumber party where they all decided to practice kissing. From what she could remember, Mary Eileen wanted to practice a few other things too, but they'd all been too scared to try them. As for the rest of the girls who ran around with them, well, if Bridget knew her budding Dykes on Bikes, they were the local chapter by now.

By the time they got ready to leave town, Bridget was pretty much resigned to the trip. It made it easier that Vic was so very obviously up to something. That was usually good. Bridget even resisted taking a peek in the toy bag when she loaded it in the car. No point in spoiling the surprise, whatever it was. At least they were staying at a hotel, so no matter what, there was a bright side.

Vic wasn't letting anything slip, though. She was too tired for sex in the hotel they stopped at halfway there, which was weird, and she wasn't talking much during the drive, which was weirder. Bridget was getting antsy and it brought out the pushy bottom in her. She wheedled, she whined, she sulked, anything to get Vic to do something with or to her—anything at all. She squirmed against the fabric of the car seat imagining a few of those things. But for the first time in years, Vic wasn't going for it. She smiled when Bridget pouted and stonewalled when she whined until her girlfriend thought she'd go nuts before they got there.

Finally, just when she thought she couldn't take another minute, they pulled into the hotel parking lot a few blocks from St. Mary's. Vic slammed her door shut and headed over to check them in without a backward glance.

Bridget took this as a good sign. It meant she was well and truly annoyed and in full top mode. Maybe Vic would spank her. She loved that, especially if she had to confess her sins beforehand. Good Catholic girls never forget their early training, as Sister Agnes used to say.

Bridget grinned, her spirits lifting as she unpacked the car.

She hauled the bags into the lobby just in time for Vic to get the key, then trailed after her up the stairs to the third floor. Evidently she hadn't earned using the elevator. She grinned in anticipation as she gasped for breath. This would be good.

But when they finally got upstairs and she got the bags lined up the way Vic liked them, her girlfriend disappeared into the bathroom to take a shower, leaving her to squirm on the bed. When she couldn't stand it anymore, she got up and checked the bathroom door. Vic had locked it. Bridget stared at it in complete disbelief and tried to think of what she'd done that was so awful.

By the time Vic came out, she was feeling contrite and just aching to atone for her sins. Especially since Vic was wearing her favorite suit, the black one that made her look hotter than... well, any other butch Bridget could think of. Vic grinned at her and grabbed one of the bags, then she gestured at the bathroom. "Go hop in the shower, then put these on when you get out. Don't put on anything else. The dance is tonight and I've got a surprise or two for you."

Bridget took the bag reluctantly, wondering whether things would be better if she groveled enough. But Vic didn't seem interested so she gave up and sulked her way into the bathroom. Even a half-hearted attempt at masturbating didn't help. Finally, she gave up and decided that she'd get seriously dolled up for the dance. That would make it up to Vic.

She was a little more optimistic when she stepped out of the shower and dried off. A few moments work with a hair dryer and she was feeling even better about the whole thing. That was when she opened the bag that Vic had given her. A puddle of plaid in green and black stared back at her and she almost shut the bag. No way. Vic couldn't have done what she thought she'd done. She reached into the bag and pulled out a Catholic school uniform. An old St. Mary's uniform, to be exact.

Under the jumper and white blouse that looked way too small for her, she found a bra with lace cups and a thong—and a pair of saddle shoes. These made her giggle. This was going to be some surprise after all. She pulled on the underwear, then the blouse. It barely buttoned across her adult breasts and the cloth gaped every time she took a deep breath, exposing the white lace bra. She pulled on the skirt and realized that it would just about cover her ass. Bridget grinned at her reflection in the mirror and grabbed her makeup.

A few moments later, a vision that would have made Sister Agnes turn over in her grave sauntered out of the bathroom to Vic's appreciative whistle. Bridget had made up her lips in a crimson that clashed violently with her red hair, then applied glowing blue eye shadow from her lashes to her eyebrows. Her hair was even done up in multiple little ponytails, just the sort of thing she might have tried in high school if she'd had the nerve.

Vic came over for an appreciative, giggly kiss. She ran one hand under the skirt and groped Bridget's ass in the thong just enough to get her attention before she pulled away. Then she grabbed a small bag from the bed, "C'mon, let's go. Some folks are waiting for us. Oh, wait, wear this." She handed Bridget a St. Mary's blazer.

Bridget gaped at it. "Where did you find all this stuff? Some kind of Sacred Heart Parish garage sale or something?"

"I had help. Now c'mon, babe. We want to get there early. I hear they're doing dinner first."

"Oh, yum, church suppers. I can't wait." Bridget rolled her eyes and tugged on the blazer. Vic was already holding the door open and ushering her out. Well, maybe the surprise would come afterward. Bridget got just a bit wetter thinking about all the possibilities.

By the time they pulled up in front of St. Mary's, the seat was getting damp under her. Not that Vic seemed to notice. She just looked as cool as could be as she pulled into the lot and came around to open Bridget's door. Bridget got out carefully, trying to hold the minuscule plaid skirt down so it sort of covered her butt. Vic watched her with a dangerous smile and leaned in close to whisper, "I'm planning on seeing a lot more of your ass and pussy tonight than that. But it's a start."

Bridget met her eyes and shivered. She'd been aching to be touched ever since her shower and that only made it worse. She wondered what it would take to get Vic to take her in the bathroom or maybe the girl's locker room. She'd always had a fantasy about that, one that involved the entire girls' field hockey team. But who knew? Maybe Vic's surprise involved her dressing up in the old team uniform. Now there was a thought.

They passed under a big banner and some streamers welcoming them to the reunion. Bridget forced herself not to groan. Crepe paper. Did it get any cheesier than that? There was Betty Crane waving at her from a registration table crowded with name tags. Bridget didn't recognize the woman next to her or the guy hovering nearby, but she suspected she'd hear all about it when they got a bit closer. And she was willing to bet that no one would ask a thing about Vic.

Sure enough, Father William and Sister Julia were fussing with more crepe paper and balloons behind the table and carefully ignoring them. Bridget tugged the jacket closed over her gaping white blouse and grabbed Vic's hand. It was time to get the evening's ostracizing underway. "Hi, Betty!" she chirped when they stopped in front of the table. "You look great." She grinned down at her least favorite former classmate and nearly collapsed laughing when she saw the look on her face.

"Hi, Bridget. You look...umm...healthy. Let me introduce you to my husband." Betty grabbed for the bored looking man who was lurking by the bulletin boards. He looked Bridget over and leered but only a little, which was better than she expected of any guy who'd marry Betty.

Vic stepped between the two of them, making it clear that she wasn't going to put up with much crap. Bridget watched Betty's uptight mouth tense as Vic reached out to shake her hand. She wondered if the reunion chair would be wiping her hand off on her skirt under the table. At least the husband was polite about it.

But a few other classmates came up behind them, and they were able to move on before Bridget could give Betty a piece of her mind. Maybe, she thought as Vic towed her away, tonight would be a good night to tell Father William who had tried to out a third of the class with anonymous notes her senior year. She'd always suspected it was Betty, partially because a lot of the accusations had been wrong.

But once they walked inside, she forgot all about her former foe. There was Monica waving at them from a side table, black hair cut short and spiky, black leather jacket draped on the back of her chair. There was another woman with her who looked familiar, too. It took Bridget a full minute to recognize Mary Eileen. Who else would wear an outfit that looked suspiciously like an updated version of a field hockey uniform? Bridget was giggling when they sat down next to them. A few more friends from the old days and their girlfriends straggled in after that so it made for a full table.

In the end, there were eight of them, including almost every girl Bridget had ever wondered about when they were in school together: Monica, Mary Eileen, Sharon, Elena, Kate, plus Vic and Kate's girlfriend Pam. She wondered what Sister Agnes would make of them now, but she thought she knew the answer to that one. At least dinner was better than she expected and everyone at the table was being very nice to Vic. Especially since it turned out that Vic seemed to know Monica and Elena from some email list, which was news to Bridget.

But apart from that, Bridget was still waiting to be surprised. Sure, Vic's hand was resting on her thigh under the table, but it wasn't working its way up like she expected. She wondered if anyone would notice if she ducked under the table and went down on her girlfriend. Probably, with this crowd. She wriggled impatiently.

Vic leaned over to whisper, "Meet me in the girl's locker room in ten minutes." Then she got up and took off with Monica.

Bridget looked after them like a lost puppy as they walked away. A wet, empty puppy whose thong was working its way up into places that wanted to be full of other things. Ten minutes had never taken so long, but she wanted to stay on Vic's good side so she didn't get up until nine and one half minutes after Vic and Monica had left.

She caught Mary Eileen's knowing smile from the corner of her eye and pulled her friend's hair lightly as she walked past, for old time's sake. Then she made herself walk across the gym at a slow ladylike pace toward the locker rooms, occasionally waving to an old schoolmate not too appalled to acknowledge her.

Eventually, she made it to the locker room door. It was shut and she stopped in front of it, letting her fantasies run wild. She slipped the blazer off her shoulders and unbuttoned her blouse an extra button or two. Then she walked in, pussy muscles clenched tight with anticipation.

The second she walked in, someone dropped a bag of some kind over her head. Her arms were held behind her back, and she was marched over to what felt like a post. She could feel her hands being securely fastened behind her around the post while someone gave her nipple a wicked pinch.

Bridget whimpered happily and spread her legs, the cheerful grin on her face hidden by the black bag. A sharp slap with something—a ruler?—on her bare thigh made the grin go away a second after it appeared. Rough hands tugged off the bag leaving her face to face with Monica, who kissed her hard.

Uh-oh. Hope Vic doesn't see this. Monica's hand was squeezing her tit now, too, with enough pressure to make her yelp around Monica's tongue in her mouth. Then Monica let go of her boob and stuck her hand between Bridget's legs, driving her fingers up around the thong until Bridget was gasping for air. "You were always such a little slut, Bridge. Now lick my fingers off." Monica added that last command right after she pulled her fingers out of Bridget's soaking pussy.

"I remember," Monica purred as she watched Bridget carefully suck off each finger on her right hand, "how you were always hanging out here after field hockey practice. What were you hoping for back then, Bridge?"

Bridget responded with an incoherent gurgle. How had Monica known? Monica wasn't telling, but she was pulling a largish knife out of her back pocket. She ran the blade down Bridget's ample cleavage and smiled as she squirmed. Bridget was wild eyed; where was Vic? Surely she hadn't left her alone with this crazy woman?

"Well, don't carve her up before I've had any." Mary Eileen

swept into the locker room, giving Bridget an evil grin. She leaned over and bit Bridget's nipple through the lace of her bra. Bridget yelped. Mary Eileen glanced at Monica. "You bring the ruler? Excellent. I've got my old field hockey stick, too."

Bridget's eyes bulged. There was no way Mary Eileen was going to follow through on that unspoken threat. But Mary Eileen pulled a condom out of a bag and opened the package. Then she stretched it over the handle of the stick. She looked up and met Bridget's wide-eyed stare. "Oh, don't tell us you didn't dream about this back in the day, sweetie. I remember you practically humping Monica in her uniform when you'd had a few beers."

So could Bridget. Who could help it? Monica had been so hot. Come to think of it, so had Mary Eileen. And now she was going to get some of her favorite fantasies fulfilled. At least she hoped they were still favorites. She hadn't thought about the field hockey team in quite a few years, not since Vic came along. She closed her eyes and pictured Vic as the team goalie and a thin line of wetness ran down her thigh.

"I'd put that on her now," Mary Eileen murmured to Monica as she ran a hand up Bridget's thigh and stuck two of her fingers inside her, then pulled them out. "I'm guessing our little Bridget's a shrieker, aren't you, sweetie?"

Bridget nodded like her head was on strings. Monica reached into a bag and came back with a thick, silky scarf in her hands. She covered Bridget's mouth and tied the scarf behind her head with deft precision. Then she pulled up Bridget's skirt and cut the thong off her. Bridget moaned, hoping that might be enough to get one of them to take her. She had never felt so empty.

Instead, Monica chuckled in her ear before running her tongue all the way down to her cleavage. She unfastened the bra and pulled it down so Bridget's breasts were exposed. Bridget started breathing faster. This was just like her field hockey fantasy. Vic had to be somewhere nearby, planning this whole thing. She was the only one Bridget had ever told about this. She squirmed happily. This was going to be the best belated birthday present ever.

The door swung open just as Mary Eileen braced the hockey stick on the floor and started working the edge of the handle up into Bridget's pussy. The smooth hardness of it stretched her out enough that she was making a whole series of protesting noises as the rest of their friends walked in. Elena gave Bridget a nasty grin as she sauntered up. "Our little hockey club slut is finally getting her wish, huh?" She reached around Bridget and slipped a finger up Bridget's ass just as Mary Eileen finally got the stick at a good angle. Elena leaned in and bit down on the tender skin over Bridget's collarbone.

Bridget writhed, every motion driving the stick a little farther inside her. Elena was giving her one hell of a hickey from the feel of things. She had also dropped her free hand to Bridget's clit. The others were either watching or starting to entertain themselves; Kate's girlfriend already had her shirt off and Kate stretched out on one of the locker room benches. Bridget found herself imagining Sister Agnes watching and surprised herself by coming with a muffled yell.

Elena grinned and pushed her legs farther apart. Then she twisted the hockey stick a little into her. It was too big to fit much more than the end, but that wasn't stopping her from trying. Bridget opened her eyes at the sound of a camera click. Monica was taking pictures of them. Elena leaned in close to Bridget's face and grinned at the camera while she pinched Bridget's nipples completely erect. Monica zoomed in on a close-up of the stick as Bridget wailed through the gag.

The door swung open behind Monica, and Bridget gasped

as a nun entered. Elena stepped away, an evil grin on her face. Bridget braced herself for outraged cries, threats to call the police, something that would bring this scene to a crashing halt. Instead the nun looked her straight in the eye and walked over, pulling a ruler out of her sleeve as she approached. Bridget gurgled behind the gag, gasping in shock at the sight of Vic in full Catholic drag, heavy rosary and all.

She was in full character, too. She looked at Bridget sternly and asked in a voice slightly deeper than her normal one, "Have you been tempting these innocents into sin? Have you? Have you exposed yourself in order to make your schoolmates think lustful thoughts?" Vic frowned fiercely as Bridget tried to look innocent.

Whack! The ruler landed on her bare thigh. Bridget yelled through the gag. Vic pulled the hockey stick away from her pussy. "I still can't hear you, Miss O'Halloran. Perhaps this will help loosen your tongue." Vic yanked off her rosary and began stuffing it up into Bridget's soaking wet slit. When she had gotten as many beads inside her as she could fit, Vic found a stray length to stuff up her ass. Bridget could feel the crucifix dangling between her thighs, and it made her feel incredibly sacrilegious.

It also made her come again, this time so hard she would have dropped to the floor if her bound hands hadn't been holding her up. "Did I give you permission to indulge in that disgusting behavior?" Vic hissed the words as the ruler met the exposed flesh of Bridget's ass. Her eyelids flew open in time to see Sharon going down on Mary Eileen while Monica slid a dildo into a harness. Vic twisted the rosary inside her and rubbed one of the dangling beads against her clit while she watched them. Whenever she felt Bridget wasn't paying enough attention, she brought the ruler down on her ass or thighs.

Bridget was gulping the air like it was water now, her knees trembling. The pressure on her clit was unrelenting as she watched Sharon come, face still pressed into Mary Eileen's pussy. Bridget joined her a second later, shaking so hard that Vic had to catch her. Vic untied her then and pulled the gag off. Then she yanked the rosary out. "I believe that you need to do some penance, young lady." She pressed down on Bridget's shoulders, and Bridget dropped to her knees on the locker room floor.

For a wild minute, she pretended she was going down on Sister Agnes. She closed her eyes, imagining the spanking she'd have gotten for this. A sharp slap just like the one she'd been thinking about cracked across her naked ass. Eyes wide, she tried to glance around to see who the hand belonged to, only to have Vic hold her head in place and order her to lick harder.

Whoever was spanking her was a pro. A firm hand came down over and over until Bridget's ass was hot and her thighs were soaked. Then she felt the pressure of a dildo against her asshole. Monica. It had to be Monica. She was going to get Vic and Monica at the same time? This *was* the best birthday present ever.

She licked Vic fiercely as Monica stretched her out and shoved her way inside. Vic came then, hands buried in Bridget's hair, legs shaking around her ears. Monica worked the dildo all the way inside and began riding her, driving Bridget's face into Vic with each thrust. Bridget tried to make her tongue rigid, using it to fuck Vic until her girlfriend came again.

Monica was groaning now and Bridget could feel her playing with herself. Monica came before she did, collapsing on Bridget's back with a shuddering yell as Bridget's legs trembled from her own orgasm. She shook under Monica's body for another minute or two then started laughing. She grinned up at Vic from the floor and said, "Should I say ten Hail Marys as penance, Sister?"

Vic gave her a stern frown. "Make it twenty and I want to hear every one of them, young lady." Bridget dropped back onto her knees and clasped her hands, beginning the litany and making sure to work in a new section thanking the Virgin for the field hockey team.

A MIDWINTER NIGHT'S DREAM

Fran Walker

In between Imlay City and Marlette, there's nothing to see on State Highway 53 but endless acres of fields punctuated by the occasional stand of trees. Though it's past dusk, no house lights show. The snow-covered farmland appears barren and desolate. It looks the way you feel: empty, miserable, down to your last few hundred bucks and in need of a lover. Or, better yet, a good lay, without all the disasters and angsty-wangsty drama that always seem to come with a relationship.

Money doesn't grow on trees and good no-strings-attached sex is nearly impossible to find. You remind yourself that you're on vacation, albeit the only kind you can afford: house-sitting for your sister while she and her husband and three kids go lie on the beach in Cancun. Of course, your sister's Persian cats will shed all over your clothes, her Great Dane will slobber on your face, and her oldest kid's pony will do its best to kick and bite you, but at least you'll have a quiet week in a house where the TV and stereo work and the fridge is full of food and your boss can't yell at you.

Slap-clank-clunk. Your take your foot off the accelerator. You know exactly what *slap-clank-clunk* means. Your Toyota Corolla made the same sound yesterday when you were driving home from the mall. It took you an entire day and most of your savings to get the timing belt replaced.

This time you're not just half a mile from a mechanic's shop.

The Toyota's engine sputters, then goes silent. You find your cell phone by feel in the dark as the car coasts down a hill. The readout shows one miserable bar. No coverage here.

"Hell, hell, *hell!*" You curse your rotten luck, your falling-apart old car and that traitorous mechanic who swore the new timing belt would last at least sixty thousand miles.

The car lurches toward the shoulder. Snow crunches under the tires. You wrench the car back onto the road in a movement that burns the muscles in your wrists and arms. Without power, the steering wheel suddenly weighs a ton. You glance around: Dark empty fields. Dark tree-shaped clumps of shadow. And a light—

You grip the heavy steering wheel harder. It's a round, yellow backlit sign that says *HELL* in red letters.

"I knew it," you mutter. Then, as you near the sign, you can see it more clearly and your heart thumps. The *S* on the sign has been smashed out. *SHELL*, it should read.

Your breath whooshes out in a sigh of relief. Not hell after all, but a gas station. Divine intervention. Maybe there really is a god.

The car coasts into the gas station so slowly you barely need to touch the brakes to park it beside the pump nearest the road. The station's store windows are shuttered, but light pokes through the slats. And there are other cars in the parking lot—an old clunker like your Toyota by the far pump and an

SUV with the gas nozzle stuck in its tank. You mutter disjointed prayers to the deity you don't believe in as you get out of the car and pop the hood.

The broken *SHELL* sign provides enough light that you can see a timing belt lying loose on top of the engine. You pick up the notched rubber belt, frowning. It's unbroken. It doesn't take a car expert to know that this isn't possible. The belt could only fall off if it broke. How many timing belts could that useless overpriced mechanic have stuffed in there?

You bend over and peer into the engine. There's the camshaft. There's the crankshaft. No timing belt. You look again at the unbroken belt in your hand. The people in the Shell station are going to think you're crazy.

A bell on the door tinkles as you push it open and hurry into the warmth. There's no one in the tiny store, just a small rack of candy bars beside a counter with a cash register and a doorway to another room through which light and soft music spill.

You walk forward carrying the timing belt, then stop in the doorway to the next room. Behind a long bar, a strikingly pretty black woman with microbraids down to her waist fills mugs from a beer tap and hands one to a denim-clad woman waiting at the bar. Two men in flannel shirts lean over the pool table near the back of the room. A jukebox plays Patsy Cline.

Someone cries out, wailing and gasping at the same time. The black woman behind the bar smiles. The man in the red flannel shirt straightens.

You grab at the wall to steady yourself.

There's a half-naked woman lying on the pool table. She's still crying out in that wailing gasp. Blue flannel shirt has his bearded cheek leaning on her thigh, his hands between her legs. Red flannel shirt caresses the woman's breasts.

The woman sits up, sighs and begins buttoning her blouse.

Blue flannel helps her off the pool table. Red flannel bends to help her tug her skirt into place. The woman, a little tottery on her high heels, walks across the room and past you as if you're not even there. The shop door makes its tinkling sound as the woman exits. Outside, a car engine starts. Both flannel men wash their hands at a small sink in the corner of the room.

The denim-clad woman walks over to the pool table and peels off her jeans. "The gray Subaru," she says. "Fill it up with regular unleaded."

Red flannel takes the woman's beer glass and sets it on a nearby table. Blue flannel lifts her onto the pool table, then leans over and strokes her throat. You notice that red flannel is, in fact, not a man. She's got ultrashort hair and a stocky build, but she's also clearly got breasts under that red flannel shirt.

Your knees feel wobbly. You sink into a chair at a nearby table, feebly clutching at the timing belt that should not have fallen off, and wonder if the whole world has gone crazy.

The bartender comes over and silently hands you a glass of red wine.

"My car," you say, holding up the timing belt. "I had this put on new just yester—"

The bartender nods and returns to her beer taps. All you can do is watch as she polishes the long wooden bar, as blue flannel runs his tongue across the denim-woman's breasts, as red flannel swirls her fingertip around the woman's clitoris.

You watch.

Denim-woman begins to pant. So do you.

Red flannel's fingers move faster. The woman on the pool table rocks back and forth soundlessly. The pool table creaks. "Fuck me," she says.

The bartender walks over to the pool table. She unzips her black leather pants and releases a long black dildo. Your hand clenches around the timing belt. Red flannel pauses, straightens, and gestures to direct denim-woman's gaze to the bartender.

The woman glances at the dildo, then turns her head away. The bartender steps back. She starts zipping up her pants again. When she glances over and catches you staring at her cock, you gasp and look away and pretend to be drinking your wine. She smiles, unzips her leather pants again and leans back against the wall, leaving her cock jutting out at you.

Red flannel slides her fingers into the woman, who pushes down as if to take the whole hand inside herself. You squirm in your seat. Again you can't help peeking at the bartender. The rich dark skin, the long swinging braids, the leather pants and the dildo—that long, smooth, black cock.

The woman on the pool table thrashes her head back and forth. Her fingers grip the edges of the table. She looks up at blue flannel. "Touch me," she says. "Fuck me."

Red flannel, her hand between the woman's thighs, thrusts her fingers in and out. Blue flannel pulls something out of his pocket and touches it. You hear it start buzzing. He holds the little vibrator against denim-woman's clit. She thrusts her pelvis up, pushing against the vibrator while red flannel hand-fucks her.

You wriggle in your wooden chair. The seam of your pants is a welcome pressure against your own clit, which is swollen and throbbing. If denim-woman comes, you will too. You take a quick gulp of wine from your glass.

Out of the corner of your eye, you see the bartender stroking her cock. Her hand, heavy with gold rings, slides up and down the length of the shaft. You lick a drop of wine off your lips and wish you were licking the bartender's fingers instead.

She lifts her hand away from the dildo and sucks on her forefinger.

Your mouth grows dry.

She drops her hand again and cups it around the base of the dildo. You look at the sculpted tip of the dildo, willing her to touch it.

The bartender's hand slides forward. She fondles the tip of her cock, squeezing it between her forefinger and thumb.

You wonder if she's able to read your mind. You wonder what would happen if you let yourself think about a blindfold.

Sudden sound and movement drag your attention away from the bartender's dildo. Denim-woman climbs off the pool table. She must have come while you were staring at the bartender. The woman pulls on her jeans, murmurs something to the flannel shirts, and leaves.

The flannel shirts wash their hands. The bartender zips up her pants.

It's your turn.

You hold up the timing belt. "My car broke down," you say.

Blue flannel comes over and takes the belt.

"Can you put it back on?" you ask.

He nods. Your shoulders sag in relief. He looks like the kind of man who can put a timing belt on a car's crankshaft and not have it inexplicably fall off a day later. Blue flannel leaves, carrying the belt.

You could walk away. You could wait outside while blue flannel fixes your car. Or maybe the denim-lady with the Subaru could give you a ride to the next town.

You walk over to the pool table.

Your hands tremble as you unbutton your pants. You're still wet and throbbing from what you've been watching. You can smell your own desire as your pants slide down to your ankles.

Red flannel boosts you up. You sit on the pool table, the rounded wooden edge cool against your bare ass. The bartender walks around the table and stands in front of you. Slowly she unzips her leather pants. The black dildo springs out. You're barely breathing. You want to touch her cock and suck on it. You want to grab it and shove it into yourself. You're aching, throbbing, empty.

Red flannel pulls a bandana from her pocket and holds it out to you. Her hands are sturdy, like her body, blunt and thick. Her eyes, pale blue in a tanned, handsome face, ask a mute question.

You nod and close your eyes. Her strong, blunt fingers brush your face as she ties the bandana over your eyes. Those hands then close over your shoulders and slowly, gently, red flannel pulls you down until you're lying on the table. The green baize feels warm and fuzzy against your back. The strong hands lift your legs, bending them at the knees, until your heels rest on the edge of the pool table on either side of your hips. Your pants are still around your ankles, preventing you from spreading your legs any wider. Cool air flows over your exposed, pulsating cunt.

Hands slide up and down your thighs. There are rings on the fingers of those hands: It's the bartender. Your breath catches. Something prods your thigh. You can picture that dildo, long and black. It brushes your cunt, then moves up to your clit, pressing and poking, sliding through your slipperiness.

You want to clasp your legs around the bartender's waist and pull her closer. You want to reach between your legs and touch the dildo and pull it into yourself. Your ankles are shackled by your pants, but your hands are free. You reach down. You want someone to stop you. You're so wet, so ready, that you know you'll come the moment you touch the dildo.

Red flannel's hands capture your wrists and pull your arms up over your head. You tug against her. Her strong fingers tighten their grip. You can't move your arms. You scoot your ass forward, tipping your pelvis up a bit, guiding the bartender's cock into yourself.

Red flannel yanks you back. The cock slides out of you. You moan in frustration. The tip of the dildo slides back up to your clit. The bartender must be holding her cock, moving it, for it dances rapidly against your clit, jiggling the sensitive flesh, while red flannel holds you firmly in place.

Someone is crying out, "Oh, oh, oh!" You realize it's your own voice, aching, desperate, craving. Behind you, red flannel's breathing becomes fast and harsh. She clamps one large hand around both your wrists. Her other hand curves down and squeezes your nipple. In a swift, sudden move, the bartender drives her cock into you.

The long black dildo slides in with ease, while red flannel rubs and pinches your nipples. The bartender pushes deeper until the zipper on her leather pants presses firmly against your clit. She thrusts in and out. You shove yourself against her, wanting more.

Red flannel squeezes your breasts with her strong hands. The bartender plunges into you, faster and faster, while the excruciating pleasure builds and swells. With her cock in your cunt, her zipper teasing your clit and her hands clasping your thighs, you come in a pulsating explosion that seems to last forever.

Your legs tremble as you lie on the pool table, panting. Eventually red flannel helps you sit up. You pull the blindfold down, sliding it over your nose, then your chin, until it is draped around your neck. In front of you, the bartender is smiling, looking nearly as sated as you feel. Red flannel smiles, too, as she helps you climb off the table and pull your pants up.

A warm glow suffuses your entire body as you walk out of the bar. There's no sign of blue flannel in the parking lot. You climb into your Toyota. The car starts easily when you turn the key in the ignition. It's pitch-dark now. You pull out of the parking lot and back onto Highway 53. Dampness seeps through the crotch of your pants.

You glance in the rearview mirror. No lights. No *SHELL* sign. In the darkness, you can't even see the outline of the building.

Maybe it's not there. Maybe it never was.

You touch the unfamiliar bandana that's still looped around your neck.

Or maybe, you think, next week at this time you'll be driving home, and you'll need to fill up your gas tank somewhere between Marlette and Imlay City. And maybe that beautiful bartender will have a wooden paddle and handcuffs somewhere behind the bar. And if you have to wait and watch until it's your turn, well, that'll be just fine.

You drive on, smiling.

SWOLLEN

Rachel Kramer Bussel

I smiled to myself, cupping my extended belly as I boarded the plane for my flight from JFK to Oahu, grateful that I'd made the cutoff by a few weeks for pregnant women to safely fly. I needed a break, and the bleak New York winter was taking its toll on both my body and mind. Part of me still couldn't believe that I was pregnant, due to a misguided threesome with my ex, Lauren, and some guy she'd picked up for the night. I had taken part mostly to be close to her, and somehow, I was the one who wound up pregnant even though I consider myself as close to 100-percent dyke as possible. Ah, the things we do for love... She had wanted to watch me with him.

When I found out, I knew immediately I wanted to keep the baby, but Lauren wasn't so sure—about the baby, or me. She and I tried to work things out, but she wasn't ready to become a mom, and surprising even to me I was. I was firm about that from the start even though I couldn't totally articulate why.

I've never regretted my decision, though for the next five

months it meant that I was climbing-the-walls horny all the time
and had to rely on my trusty collection of vibrators. I'm a huge
fan of sex toys, but I missed the companionship of a woman,
someone who'd stroke me all over, who'd coax forth my orgasm
like she needed me to come to save her life. Someone who'd
kiss and lick and whisper to me, who'd make me feel beautiful
when I was starting to truly doubt I ever would again. But it's
hard enough to meet women, for me, anyway, let alone do so
with a rapidly expanding belly, so I'd pretty much given up on
dating. This was my last hurrah, a final chance to have fun and
bask in the sun and surf. I picked Hawaii both for the distance
and because I'd heard it was beautiful. Not that I planned to lie
outside all day, but a little sun, some nonalcoholic fruity drinks,
a chance to walk around in as little clothing as possible and bask
in my pregnant belly without a care in the world, sounded like
just what I needed.

Much as I wouldn't have picked this as the prime time to have
the most explosive sex of my life, neither would I have picked
Katherine as the woman to have it with. She certainly didn't
look like any kind of wild sexual animal when she checked me
into the hotel. "You'll be in Room One-Oh-Five, Ms. Locke,"
she said, giving me a sweet, simple smile. She was small-boned,
petite, with brown hair that simply hung in a straight line, not
the stick-straight of someone who deliberately straightens her
hair, but a natural sheath. There was no hint of flirtation when
she looked at me, and it's only in looking back that I can recall
the hand placed on my back, the simple, "If there's anything at
all you need while you're here, feel free to ask."

But isn't that what anyone working in a hotel would say to
any guest? I found out later, at three in the morning when the
bath I'd drawn had simply failed to ease the aches all over my
body, when she said "anything," she meant it. I'd brought a

vibrator, and I slipped under the soft, high-thread-count covers, grateful I'd chosen a luxury hotel rather than trying to save money. But even the vibe didn't do more than bring me temporary relief. I was antsy, so I threw on the plush white robe the hotel had kindly provided, along with my own fuzzy bunny slippers, and padded my way out into the hall. I wasn't really sure where I was going, and the still silence of the place stopped me in my tracks. New York City is never truly silent; there's always a faint rumbling of the train or cars, or late-night party animals whooping it up. The silence made me also stop and notice the delicate blue-and-yellow-flowered wallpaper. I traced my fingers over it lightly as I headed down the hall, toward a light outside.

And there was Katherine. She looked more delicate out of her uniform, wearing a simple black robe that covered her but was sheer enough to show the outline of her body. Her hair was pulled back in a ponytail, and she was reading under a lamp by the pool. "Hi," I said shyly as she looked up at me. Her face lit up and she motioned for me to come sit.

"Are we supposed to be out here?" I asked, enjoying the warm night air and the peaceful pool next to us, the ocean not far away.

"Sweetheart, we can do whatever we want," she said gently. Did I detect a hint of mischief in her voice? I thought so. She settled me onto the lounge chair she'd just been sitting on, then lowered it down. I'd found the sun too hot for me when I first arrived—maybe it was the weight from the pregnancy—but the evening air felt far more refreshing.

"Would you like a massage?" I wasn't sure if she was asking me on a professional or personal basis. I'd become so used to being on my own that having this hushed conversation felt strange, like we were breaking some kind of rule, though I couldn't really think of any we'd actually transgressed—so far.

It was then that I saw the tattoo on her wrist, the one thing that seemed to set her apart. It was a purple heart, cracked in half, the jagged inner edges captivating; I wondered why she'd want to commemorate heartbreak. We hadn't talked all that much, but once her hands settled onto my neck, I felt totally at ease. So much so that tears started to fill my eyes as her knuckles dug into me. It had been so long since I'd been really, truly touched; I got lots of friendly smiles and gallant gestures, like people letting me cut lines or take their seats on the subway, or others wanting to touch my newly sprouted belly, but real intimacy had been scarce since I heard the news. My parents had pretty much said I was on my own, though I was sure they'd change their minds, and at work I was putting in extra hours to try to prove myself worthy.

All of it had clearly taken its toll, and being in such a beautiful setting, stealing this time out of the night, with a woman's strong hands calling out to me, was just too much. Katherine didn't say anything, she just let the tears roll down my face as soft sobs traveled through me, her hands a constant on my skin. Eventually, she leaned down and brushed her lips against my neck, so gently I almost didn't realize she'd done it. But then she did it again, this time nipping my skin gently with her teeth. Her lips were saying, "I want you." It had been so long since anyone had even hinted at wanting me, I wasn't sure what to do.

"I—" I started to say, but she cut me off.

"Let me take care of you tonight. For the rest of your stay… you look like you could use some TLC. And, if you ask me, you also look absolutely beautiful," she whispered in my ear.

"Do you really think so?" I needed her reassurance, needed her to make me feel beautiful again.

"Oh, yes, and I'm going to prove it to you. Come with me," she murmured, pulling me along with her. If any guests had glanced out their window, they'd have seen one woman in a see-through black robe pulling another one with a big belly along behind her, though I was glad to follow. I purposefully didn't let myself think too much about what we were doing. I was excited, a little nervous, a lot in awe. I wasn't quite horny, though. Yet. That would come soon. Katherine guided me to a suite, one much fancier than mine and fancier than I'd have expected a worker's quarters to be. She must be someone special around here.

We walked in and she guided me to the bed, opening the blinds just enough to let in a sliver of moonlight. "Lie back, and let me take care of you," she repeated. And then she proceeded to show me just how beautiful she found me. This wasn't about falling in love or getting to know each other, about observing each nuance of body language, memorizing every detail. Well, maybe it was for Katherine. As for me, I sank back against the luxurious pile of pillows and allowed her tongue to transport me. She had started again at my neck, with kisses and licks that made me squirm, and then she moved down to my breasts. They were heavy and tender, sensitive already, but under her touch they sprang to life, returning to their former glory as she turned my nipples into beady jewels atop my large breasts. She tugged one between her teeth while twisting the other, reminding me how I used to get off on extreme nipple play with clamps. That seemed like another lifetime, but my pussy responded as Katherine's mouth and fingers respectively teased my nipples.

She could tell just what she was doing to me, and we both knew it. "Relax, Bea, relax," she urged me. I hadn't realized I'd been at all tense or uncertain until she said it. Of course I'd thought I was relaxed as I lay naked on the bed, my pregnant belly rising upward, somehow no longer heavy and uncomfortable, as a beautiful woman coaxed me halfway toward orgasm.

But when I let out a breath and sank deeper into the luxurious sheets, I realized I had been holding out, some small part of me perhaps thinking it unseemly or improper for me to be there with Katherine, so blatantly reveling in sex when I had more important things on my mind. But could there be anything more important than a woman's touch forcing me to get in touch with my body and desires?

I let out a moan as her mouth made its way lower, taking me farther from the realities of life and deeper into the world of pleasure. Her tongue traced its way over the hardness of my stomach, kissing and licking alternately before she reached my pubic hair. I hoped she wouldn't mind how unruly it had become, but she seemed to delight in it, running her fingers through my fuzz, tugging at a few of the hairs before she breathed against my sex, her lips so close, promising me their kiss. And Katherine was a woman who kept her promises. I felt like I was floating as she ran her tongue along my lower lips. She wasn't aggressive like some of the women I'd been with, and her gentleness seemed to imply that there was more passion lurking just beneath the surface. "You are heavenly," she said, her words music to my ears. I'd been growing steadily more aroused, out of control, filled with something new and exciting yet also terrifying. Katherine's mouth told me everything would be okay. Her tongue taught me that my pussy was still my own, that I could still bring a woman that special ecstasy that comes from partaking of another woman's juices. Her lips told me that she couldn't imagine a more sensuous delight than exploring my every nook and cranny.

I soon got over feeling selfish and simply enjoyed the gift she was giving me. I could still feel the baby, but she was, momentarily, secondary. It was just me and Katherine, and soon her fingers began exploring me as her tongue rested against my clit, sampling its heat but simply staying there, as if she'd pressed the pause button. "You're so wet for me," she observed, and I smiled. All my pent-up pleasure, my juices that had had seemingly nowhere to go, my longing that I'd poured into decorating and preparing, all came out in this exotic place, with a woman I still wasn't sure was real. It was as if she'd been sent to answer my prayers, one stroke at a time.

I was glad we'd come back to her suite, especially when she slipped away momentarily, only to return with a bottle of lube—that was the last thing I'd have thought to bring with me. "You're dripping, but I need more for what I have in mind," she said as I watched her pour some of the clear liquid onto her fingers. They were cool and slippery when they returned to the heat of my cunt; my needy, greedy hole. And then right away I knew what she was going to do, and while I wasn't sure I could handle it, I knew I wanted it. She curved her fingers together, pinching them all as if acting out some mime's routine, but this was all real. She pushed her fingers and thumb, wet with a combination of my cream and the bottled variety, inside, while I did my best to spread my legs and get ready. She entered me slowly and quickly, somehow, the dragging seconds making me ache all over. I didn't realize I was holding my breath until I let it out in a whoosh. I reached above me with both hands, holding on to the headboard as she sank her fingers deeper inside.

"You're so ready, Bea, my beautiful Bea." I wasn't hers exactly, but at that moment, I wanted to be, desperately. I'd become accustomed to the fact that I no longer belonged to anyone, but someone new was about to belong to me, and I thought I'd surrendered the dream of having another woman looking out for me, claiming me, marking me. That longing must have lurked somewhere deep within me, somewhere Katherine was about to find with those probing fingers. She managed to get past her wrist with ease, without even a twinge of discomfort, only tightness, fullness and my desire to have her inside me. She curled her fingers into a fist and I felt tears rush to my eyes. I was overwhelmed by the magnitude of her action, by her willingness to slow down and make love to me with her hand and her mind, rather than fuck me in a way that would have left me shaken. I was so swollen, from the inside out, doubly now, and I just let the tears flow as she rocked ever so slowly inside me, her eyes on my face the whole time.

Her fist was like a caress, a promise that no matter what happened, I would never lose the part of me that made me a woman, a dyke, a lover, even if I had no one to share that love with. Katherine wasn't promising me forever, but her hand seemed to extend into the future, the future me, the future mommy she was speaking to as if she already existed. My island beauty edged her hand along my insides until I cracked and came not just with my cunt but my entire being, bursting through the shadows that had been holding me down and emerging into a new place, one full of light and promise. "Yes, my dear girl," she whispered, "don't ever forget what your body can do." She eased out and I was mesmerized by the way she licked my juices gently from her fingers with the utmost tenderness.

She leaned down and kissed my belly, then led me into her bathroom for a bath, helping me into the warm water, guiding the sponge along my skin. Later, when I was dry and warm and once again in her bed, I asked if I could do something for her. I had a strong desire to make her come, not just to return the favor, but to see her beauty too blossom from the inside out.

"Watch me," she said, and pulled a pale pink dildo from her side drawer. Unabashedly throwing back the covers, she showed me how she makes love to herself, and I soaked in that image, memorized it for the future. Her cries of ecstatic agony, which she tried but failed to muffle in deference to her sleeping neighbors, made the baby kick. We fell asleep side by side, and for the rest of my stay, I spent my nights in her suite.

I had thought maybe we'd become pen pals and somehow overcome the distance, but when I wrote her, I never heard back. I still never forgot her, and I named my baby girl Kat in her honor. I plan to take Kat to Oahu someday, because even though it's not where she was conceived, it's where I learned that I could be both a mother and a lover.

CAMSHAFT CUTIE

Crystal Barela

The sun's rays were pressing down on the back of my neck, making it difficult to think. It was 115 degrees, and I was surrounded by miles of open desert and sagebrush. Screaming traffic raced past me on the highway. There was no pause at the site of my broken-down car. You would have thought that my sweat-drenched tank top would have given someone pause. It now left little to the imagination.

A hot breeze ruffled my skirt around my knees in an unsatisfying swirl. I squatted down in the shadow of my car in a most unladylike fashion and checked my mobile for the hundredth time, as if cell service would magically have become available.

The last town I had passed was Boron. THE BORAX CAPITAL OF THE WORLD the sign had read. I'd never heard of it before today. I guess I should be grateful that there was a town within thirty miles of where my car had coasted to a stop in front of one of the yellow call boxes that lined this stretch of highway. An hour had passed since AAA had said the tow truck was twenty minutes out, and I was on my last bottle of water. The urge to pour the now warm liquid over my head was nearly as strong as my want to chug it. I closed my eyes as I took a sip, offering up a prayer for salvation.

In answer there was the sound of gravel beneath wheels. I opened my eyes and blinked rapidly to see a tow truck sparkling like heaven in the sunlight. It took what I thought was a leisurely coast to the front of my dead vehicle.

The driver opened the door and got out, back to me. I saw baggy, nondescript, blue workman coveralls and an orange baseball cap. The bill, facing me, read, RIPE PEACHES.

"AAA said half an hour," I said, coming up to the driver, ready to tear him a new one.

"I got here as fast as I could, sugar," the driver said. I could hear the laughter in her voice as she turned to greet me. "We were closed when I got the call."

She had the greenest eyes I had ever seen, framed by delicate crow's feet. Shorter than I am, she squinted up at me now, giving evidence that their creation had been from the sun and not her age. The oval name patch over her left breast pocket identified her as DICK. Something shifted inside me. Anger was gone and desire now present.

"Thought I'd do ya a good Samaritan seeing as you are from out of town and all."

"Thank you," I said. "It's just so hot."

"Yes, it is," she said. Her eyes did not reach mine but instead focused on my breasts. My nipples could be seen through the thin fabric, and her pointed stare only brought them to greater attention.

Dick asked me to pop the hood. She unzipped her coveralls, letting them fall to her waist. She wore a white wife-beater. Sleeves of brightly colored tattoos ran up both arms. When she bent under the hood the coveralls tightened across what appeared to be a very firm ass. She wiggled the spark plugs and poked the battery.

I leaned in beside her, not seeing anything that appeared out of place. It looked like an engine to me.

"You said she coasted to a stop?" Dick asked, turning to me.

There was a bead of perspiration on her upper lip. She had a full bow-shaped mouth that didn't go with her garage girl look, A touch of femininity in a face of soft angles and tan skin.

"There wasn't any noise?" Dick asked.

She licked her upper lip, catching the salty drop on her tongue. The heat of the desert faded as a different heat spread through my lower body.

"Hello?" She laughed and waved a hand in front of my face.

"What?" I jumped and blushed as if I were a different kind of girl. The kind who wouldn't even consider where my imagination was taking me.

"We need to get you out of the sun," she said, and took my elbow to pull me away from the vehicle. She closed the hood.

"What's wrong with it?" It was only my elbow, I told myself. The most nonerogenous zone in the body, and I was feeling a little weak in the knees.

She pulled a red bandana from her back pocket and wiped her brow. "Well, sugar," she said, rocking back on the heels of her work boots, "I have to get inside her and make a proper inspection."

Again my cheeks heated at where my mind headed with those words.

"You're looking flushed," Dick said, putting her arm around my waist and leading me over to her truck. "Why don't you sit in the AC while I hook up your car?"

The truck was more than a step up, and she gave me a lift

with a firm hand on my ass. I gave up trying to control my perverted thoughts. More than my face was heating.

Dick reached behind the passenger seat and pulled out a bottle of ice-cold water and handed it to me. "Take a sip of that, sugar."

The air-conditioning blew my limp red hair around my head, and I lifted the bottle dutifully to my lips.

"That's nice," she said, lifting her thumb to my lip to catch some excess water. Our eyes locked and I was sure she could see the sparks in my brown ones. "I'll have you all fixed up real soon."

And then she shut the door, breaking the spell. I giggled nervously and pressed the cold bottle to my forehead. My thoughts should be far from sexual considering the situation I was in. More important than my libido was how I was going to pay for this repair, whatever it was. I had left Washington with barely enough money to make the trip to Arizona.

I could hear gears being turned behind the tow truck. There was country music on the radio, a woman's sultry alto. The cab was spotless. An air freshener in the shape of pinup girl hung from the rearview mirror, spinning slowly in the cool breeze of the AC.

Dick pulled open the driver's-side door and said, "All right, sweetness, it's time to take you home."

She climbed in gracefully and shifted the truck into gear before stretching one arm across the seat behind me. She eased the car onto the highway. Her fingernails had grease beneath them, and there was a delicate webbing of grease in the lines of her knuckles. I wondered if her fingers ever really came clean. She didn't wear a bra; it really wasn't necessary. Her breasts were small beneath her tank, and if I was not mistaken the left one was pierced.

It had been too long since my last woman, but I was still surprised by my body's response to this girl. I crossed my legs under my skirt to ease the growing ache. She was really too skinny to get me going like this. I liked my women full through the hips and ass with breasts I could drown in.

"Is Dick your real name?" I asked.

"That's something I hope you'll find out for yourself," she said, a smile in her voice. She didn't take her eyes off the road when she said it, but I felt her arm drop from the back of the seat onto my shoulders. Her fingers moved in slow circles on the bare skin of my collarbone. She began singing the lyrics to the song on the radio, terribly off-key.

By the time we pulled into the gravel lot in front of the shop the sun was starting to set, and I had almost forgotten why I was sitting next to this girl. A neon sign glowed in the window flashing DICK'S GARAGE. She led me inside and told me she was going to go unhook the car, to have a seat, and that there were cold drinks in the fridge.

The shop was filthy, grease caught in every corner and crevice like the lines in the knuckles of Dick's fingers. Posters of pinups from another era were tacked to the walls in between postings of proper vehicle maintenance and hot rods. A ratty red couch faced the door, full of holes. The stuffing peeked out of the cushion corners. Against one wall sat an old refrigerator from the '50s, white and domed. It hummed loudly. The door handle hung at an odd angle and rattled.

Opposite the fridge was a neatly organized desk with a metal folding chair in front of it. I took a seat. A cracked window was at the back of the shop, so filthy with grime that you could hardly see through it. A sign caught my attention. It dominated the full length of the desk. It read: ALL REPAIRS IN CASH UNLESS SOME OTHER ARRANGEMENTS ARE MADE IN ADVANCE—NO

VEHICLES WILL BE RELEASED UNTIL PAID IN FULL. Cash only? I cursed beneath my breath as I had been hoping that the repair would be less than five hundred dollars so it could fit on what was left of my last credit card.

The jingle of the bells on the door handle preceded Dick as she walked into the shop. She came around the desk and threw her baseball cap across the worn, speckled Formica. She sat in a chair covered in cracked turquoise vinyl, her legs spread. She ran a hand through her short, dark hair, making it stand on end and my clit harden to attention.

"Sugar, we have a problem," she said.

"More than one," I said, resting my forearms on the desk. My biceps framed my breasts in what I hoped was an attractive manner.

"First: as much as I would like to help you out, the shop is closed for the night," she said. "My guys have gone home, and I have a pretty good notion your timing belt has gone out."

"Timing belt?"

"Yes. The only way I am gonna know for sure is if I get inside her to take a look."

"Her?" Again my mind was on my heated insides.

"The engine."

"Oh."

She raised a brow at my dumbstruck expression but continued. "It's a big project involving taking apart that engine."

"Oh," I said again. I felt like an idiot. I had no idea what she was talking about. My only thoughts were on the skin I hadn't seen. Was it tattooed as well?

Dick pulled out a piece of paper and asked me for my last name. The first name was Amy, right?

I nodded. She looked at me as though she was beginning to think I was simple and not the attractive, irresistible woman who wanted to barter her body for auto repairs that I was trying to project.

"It's seventy-five dollars to check her out and make a diagnosis. I won't know how much the rest will cost until I examine her."

"Examine me?" I asked.

"You have a one-track mind, sugar," she said, her lips twitching up at the corners.

"What track is it on?"

She reached a hand over the desk and brushed a strand of my sweaty hair behind my ear. "You've been eyeing me like I was a naked call girl since I pulled up in my rig."

Even though I had been planning to offer my body for services rendered I was offended.

"Don't pout now," she said, placing her calloused thumb on my lower lip. She rubbed the sensitive flesh and my tongue snuck out for a little taste of salt and service.

"Now, sugar," Dick said as my lips closed around her thumb and sucked it into my mouth. She swallowed hard. "I don't want to presume anything."

"I don't have any cash," I mumbled around her flesh. Which was the truth.

"I'd like to..." I took her thumb from my mouth and stood with her hand in mine and walked around the desk.

I stopped between her splayed legs.

I placed her hand on my trembling stomach.

Our eyes locked. The heat in mine reflected back at me.

I slid her palm beneath the elastic of my skirt and drew her fingers against wet ivory lace. "I'd like to...make other arrangements."

Dick held her finger against the delicate fabric, pressing into my damp slit.

My knees buckled and she caught me with one strong arm.

"Get up here, sugar," she told me.

I didn't hesitate. I pulled my skirt up around my thighs and straddled her on the chair. Her hand moved with me, slipping past my panties and into my slippery insides. I moaned, leaning down to nibble at her mouth. Dick tasted like the gum she had been chewing, minty and sweet, with an under-layer of smoke, as if she had snuck a cigarette earlier in the day but was trying to quit. Her tongue was fast and caressed mine in a way that had my pussy massaging her fingers.

Her free hand was tugging at my tank top, and I leaned back to pull it over my head.

"Beautiful," she said, and I placed my hands on the back of the chair and leaned forward so she could show her appreciation properly. My full breasts were treated to her nuzzles and swipes of tongue. She drew a nipple into her mouth and sucked.

"Like that, do ya?" she mumbled as she moved to the other. My pussy tightened again as she fed.

I did like it. She was three fingers deep, her thumb thrumming my clit like a well-tuned engine.

Dick's free hand had found its way under my skirt and squeezed my ass. Her dirty little fingers slid along the crack and took a firm hold before she stood and positioned me on the desk.

Neat stacks of papers scattered and a soup can full of pens crashed to the floor. Her coveralls fell to her ankles. She wore white striped boxers and...I blinked as Dick pushed my skirt up around my waist. Her namesake winked at me through the opening of her boxers.

"You're packing," I gasped, reaching for her black rubber dick. She slapped my hands away. My pulsing pussy throbbed. I wanted her in me again.

Dick pulled her wife-beater over her head. Her tats spread in between her breasts and disappeared under her boxers, a riot of red and black and yellow and turquoise. Pinups winked at me from every direction. She twisted the silver bar in her nipple as her eyes ate me. Her skin was tan, like she went without a shirt in the desert sun. She didn't take off her boxers but reached her hand in through the front flap and pulled the rubber cock out to meet me. It was long and thick with realistic veins running its length.

Her hand was wet with my juices.

She stroked herself.

I spread my legs.

Dick pulled the bar in her nipple.

I wet my lips.

She pumped again, the black head peeking through her tan fingers.

I begged. My hand slipped between my thighs.

She told me no. I froze, short of breath, lightheaded with desire.

Dick stepped forward, dick in hand. She nudged the head against my hole. She gave a twist, entered an inch, two. I wrapped my legs around her waist and pulled her to me. I wanted all of her. She lay down against me with her full weight. In one fluid motion Dick slid through my wet cunt with her well-oiled camshaft.

We were flush, belly to belly, breast to breast. She shut her eyes and kissed me softly. Her tongue traced my lips while she rocked her hips. She went slow where I wanted fast, stroking my engine, not gunning it, pulling a purring hum from inside me. This was a scenic test drive, her movements told me, her hands running over my hills and valleys. This was discovery, her lips said, as they tasted the salty crease where my neck met shoulder.

A hand was between us. On me.

Rubbing my clit with her strong thumb.

The other held a handful of my breast, twisting the flesh toward her mouth. She sucked my nipple hard.

Twisted her key into my ignition.

And gunned me.

Fucked me from zero to sixty in thirty seconds flat.

Our cries echoed off the walls as we crossed the finish line.

It was silent aside from our gasps.

Dick chuckled and buried her head between my breasts. I could feel her smile against my skin as she kissed her way back to my mouth.

"What?" I mumbled against her lips.

She stood, pulling me with her. I sat on the edge of the desk and wrapped my legs around her waist. My forearms rested on her shoulders. I clasped my fingers loosely together. My skin was so pale next to Dick's tan and colored skin. I leaned down and took the bar through her nipple in my mouth and tugged playfully. She gasped. I smiled.

"It's just that I leave that sign up as a joke, sugar."

"What?" I asked, looking up at her through my lashes.

"You really thought I don't accept credit cards?"

"You sneaky bastard," I growled, biting at her.

She lifted me and walked around her desk.

"Where are we going?"

"I think I need another down payment," Dick said, and threw me over her shoulder.

AUGUST CRAZIES

Miel Rose

My fan had fallen out the window the week before and the air was thick and heavy. I didn't want to move, but was filled with this August restlessness, worse than any spring fever I'd ever experienced. It had me wanting to claw out of my own skin. It had me collapsed on my bed holding a bandana full of melting ice to my forehead, wishing Bren was getting home tonight and would come over and fuck the shit out of me.

It had me regretting living in a town too small for dyke bars where I could go and feel anonymous. Instead, I was stuck with coffeehouse lesbo folk nights where all my friends and most of my lovers past, present and possibly future would be congregating tonight. I had been debating whether to go or not for an hour and it was suddenly too much.

"How fucking boring!" I said this out loud and propelled myself off the bed with a force that would have surprised anyone who'd been watching me a second before. My indecision was getting on my nerves as much as the heat. I grabbed a towel and headed for the bathroom, sweaty and naked, my thighs sticking together with each step.

I slammed the door to the bathroom, not that there was anyone home to hear it. Teresa was at work, and Em was as out of town as Bren was. "Fucking Bren," I muttered, turning the shower on and adjusting it a little warmer than cold. What's the use of having a lover if she isn't there to fuck you senseless when the August heat is making you crazy? I stepped into the shower and gasped as the cold hit my chest and ran down my body. My nipples turned to hard little pits and I squeezed them roughly, thinking about Bren's biggest cock and how I wished she were here to fuck my face with it till I choked. Damn, tomorrow was too far away.

I could see if Hawk was free for a date later, but as good as it would feel to beat the shit out of her right now, what I really needed was for someone to beat me. Hawk would hit me if I asked her, but it was different than getting beat by a top. There would be none of the hard-core domination that I craved to go along with my bruises. "FUCKING BREN!" I yelled into the streaming water.

I washed quickly and got out of the shower. I had about an hour before people would be showing up at the cafe, plenty of time to get decked out. If I couldn't get the fucking I needed, at least I could make everyone there wish they were coming home with me. I started laughing at that thought and almost tripped on the stairs up to my room. I had known everyone in this town for years, and if there was any attraction, it had been negotiated already.

Maybe a date with Hawk wouldn't be such a bad idea, I mused, going through my closet. But I knew better. Hawk was an excellent lay but was too submissive to give me what I needed tonight. All her cocky little-boy attitude flew out the window the minute I started topping her. The guy wanted to get bossed around. This was hot, but it would feel like work tonight. Mostly our dates were about me hurting and fucking her, and going there would give me the worst case of blue balls. Fuck anyone who says femmes can't get blue balls.

To my surprise, the music had already started and almost everyone was there by the time I reached the cafe. Hawk and Teresa were outside smoking when I walked up, and I could hear the acoustic guitar through the walls.

"Damn, roommate," Teresa said, spotting me first, "You look fine."

She was looking pretty fine herself, clad in a short skirt and a tube top exposing the beautifully inked tattoos of red bee balm covering her chest and shoulders.

"Hey, love," I said as she rose and gave me a kiss. "How was work?"

"Stupid and boring per usual." She stubbed out her cigarette and smiled to let me know she was just bitching, that her day hadn't been that bad. She gave me a hug, maneuvering herself toward the door. "I gotta piss, baby. I'll see you inside."

Hawk was still smoking and she gazed at me with barely concealed lust. She looked like she'd come straight from work. She worked in her uncle's garage on the weekends, doing oil changes and learning mechanics, and her pants were covered with petroleum and grime. I wanted to climb onto her filthy jean-covered lap and hump her till I was coming out my ears. Instead, I sat down next to her, kissed her cheek, and ran my fingers through her short sweat-damp curls.

"How are you doing, sweetheart?" I could see a definite blush creeping across her cheeks. Too fucking cute. I wanted to drag her into the bushes and kick her ass right there.

She looked at me shyly from under her lashes. "I'm fine...
how are you?" She took my hand and brought it to her mouth,
kissing my fingers with soft dry lips. It was all I could do not to
go for her throat.

"I'm crazy, baby. I'm going totally insane. The heat is making
me tired and cranky and horny. I don't feel comfortable in my
own skin, I feel lethargic but totally manic at the same time." I
felt a small tremor go through her at the word "horny,"

"Is there anything I can do for you?" She looked at me with
hopeful eyes.

"No, baby." I took her face between my hands and kissed her
softly on the lips. "Just be sweet to me tonight. I can't take this
mood out on you; it would end bad. You're so fucking tempting
though." I grabbed the short hairs at the base of her skull, tugged
gently and then let her go.

She relaxed and reached for her tobacco. Reading my mood
like the excellent bottom she was, she asked, "When's Bren
coming home?"

"I don't know, sometime tomorrow I think." I felt distracted
and like I had to get away from her before I changed my mind
and dragged her into some corner to fuck.

Rolling her next smoke she said, "Maybe you should go
inside and get a beer, try to relax."

I kissed her cheek again, wiped off the trace of lipstick and
got up to go inside. The woman on the low stage was playing
a haunting song and crooning about lost love. I decided to
give in to the downer part of my mood and sat next to Teresa,
set on brooding and soaking up the music. I briefly fantasized
that some handsome butch from out of town would be playing
tonight and need a place to stay, but everyone was from the area,
no surprises. Besides, sleeping with someone who didn't know
me when I was in this mood would be a horrible idea.

Teresa got up to get some tea and I looked around the room to see who else was here. I saw Teresa get in line and out of the corner of my eye saw her grinning and waving at someone behind me. I craned my neck to see who she was waving at and the bottom fell out of my stomach.

"Bren! What the fuck are you doing here?"

She chuckled softly and shook her head. "Such language out of such a pretty mouth. Come back here and say hi to me."

I rose and stumbled to her seat, trying to decide in my muddled brain whether I wanted to make a scene and throw myself on her lap. I settled for sitting down next to her as close to her body as I could get. She wrapped her arms around me and I buried my face in her neck.

"Did you miss me, angel?" Her words were husky with tenderness and suddenly I wanted to break down and sob.

She leaned in close to kiss my lips but some bratty, angst-ridden part of me said, "Don't fuck up my lipstick."

She gave me a look of utter disgust and rolled her eyes. "Baby, I'm your butch. If I fuck up your lipstick, it will be intentional." Then she leaned in and kissed me so sweetly it made my connective tissue dissolve, and all my bones clattered to the floor.

Leaning back, she licked her lips, erasing any sign of my lipstick, regarded me and said, "Perfect."

"Darling, do you really want to stay for the rest of this show?" I ran my hand along her collarbone just under her shirt. I wanted to be next to her bare skin so bad.

"Uh-uh, you?" She was smiling at me like she had followed all my frustrated thoughts that day.

"No." I shook my head emphatically.

"We could go to the bar and get a drink." Her knowing smile was infuriating as her fingers traced lightly across my jaw. She was fucking with me and I wasn't in the mood.

I leaned close to her ear and dug my nails into her neck. "I want you to bring me home, beat my ass, fuck me and then suck my pussy till I come in your mouth." Call me bossy, but I had to show her my need was serious.

In one smooth movement she stood up, reached for my hand and said, "Shall we?" I let myself be guided out the door.

I caught a glimpse of Hawk on my way out. She was standing with her primary lover, an older butch named Toni, and she flashed me a sweet knowing smile seeing me leave on Bren's arm. It's funny having bottom solidarity with someone you top. It can be mind-boggling, the complexities of identity, desire, and where they intersect in alternative relationships. It can make you pull your hair out in frustration, make your heart break from all kinds of nasty feelings as we try to rewrite the horrible stories we were raised with. But when it works, when the puzzle clicks together, when everyone involved feels respected and taken care of, it can create a kind of triumph that leaves you high for years.

I blew Hawk a kiss.

Bren was all nonchalant warmth on the walk home, telling me about her trip, asking what I'd been up to. I would have been fooled, except I knew her, and I could feel the tension coiled in her muscles, emanating off her body. Damn, she was smooth though.

We walked in the door and she asked, innocently, "Is Em home?"

"No, Em's still—" I said, right before she grabbed me and slammed me hard into the wall. I felt all my breath leave my lungs in a squeak.

"Good, then your roommates won't have to hear you scream." Her voice was warm and smooth, but her eyes were hard and I could see the muscles in her jaw twitch. Her fingers were digging into my upper arms so hard they would leave bruises. I whimpered, overcome with the intensity between us, overcome by how fucking scary she got in this mode.

Her body pressed me to the wall and she grabbed my throat, squeezing hard. "You greedy little bitch. Five minutes home and already you're bitching at me to fuck you, suck you, beat you. You're such a selfish little slut."

She looked at me out of hard eyes, breathing deep. A cruel smile twisted her lips and she slowly ran her thumb over my mouth, smearing my lipstick across my face. I felt blood rush to my cheeks and my eyes narrowed.

"Get up to your room." Any warmth was gone from her words, and she grabbed me roughly and threw me toward the stairway. I stumbled in my heels, and she viciously pushed me forward. The heat hit me like a wave at the top of the stairs, making it hard to breathe. She marched me over to my loft bed, which was a perfect height to bend me over.

I was shaking and whimpering by the time she pulled my dress up and ripped my panties down the middle of my thighs. I couldn't see her, but I could hear her trying to control her breath. Then I felt her hand on my ass and my shakes became violent. She reached between my legs and grabbed the crotch of my underwear, pulling it toward her till the lace cut into my thighs.

"What's the matter, baby, are you cold?" Her other hand trailed down my shaking back. She leaned down to my ear, twisting the panties in her fist, and said between clenched teeth, "Or are you just scared to get what you asked for?" She pushed up off the bed. I could hear her unbuckling her belt, sliding it from the loops. In the midst of August heat, my teeth started to chatter.

"Tell me your safeword," she demanded.

"Uncle," I stammered. So far our age play had not included uncle/niece dynamics, and *uncle* had always been my safeword wrestling with my brothers growing up. It was easy to remember, ingrained.

"Do you want to use it?" she asked.

I shook my head emphatically and felt her hand grip my hair, wrenching my head up and twisting it slightly till our eyes met.

"I said: do you want to use it." Her voice was calm, deadly smooth, but she punctuated her words with vicious shakes of my head.

Through trembling jaws I said, "No, Sir." She was definitely Sir tonight; there was none of my daddy's tenderness in her words or actions.

My answer was evidently accepted, because with a final shake that left me dizzy, she released my head and brought the belt down with a loud crack. No warm-up, no foreplay, she brought the leather down hard. I jumped with each hit, the pain too much, too fast, making me tense up, making it hurt more. I tried to relax into it, but despite my talk, I wasn't all that used to all-out beatings with no preliminary. I tried to count her strokes in my head but couldn't concentrate. I tried to breathe through my whimpers but felt like I was hyperventilating. I tried to ground myself, tried to send my energy down, and in the center of the craziness I found calm reassurance that I was getting exactly what I needed.

"Fuck, I love beating your ass. I love how fast you welt up, how fast you start bruising. I love how your ass jiggles and shakes every time the belt hits you." Her words were colored with passion and the exertion of the beating. She was gradually moving from the top of my ass down, her strokes overlapping. When she got to the juncture between my ass and my thighs the vibrations of each hit made my pussy burn. That's when I realized I was wet, so wet, dripping down my thighs. My endorphins must have been kicking in because the pain was starting to feel good, different from the good of pain just for pain's sake that I had been craving that day. I started relaxing and rocking into the hits, my whimpers transforming to moans.

"That's it, cunt. Rock that hot ass back for me." She brought the belt down harder than she'd ever hit me, three times, one on top of the other, where the curve of my ass turns to leg. It ripped me out of my pleasure haze and sobs welled up in my throat. It took me a second to realize she had stopped hitting me, and I jumped when I felt her fingertips tracing my welts.

"Oh, sweet love. I'm so lucky to have a girl like you," she crooned. Who was she now? Was this my daddy talking? Her fingers traced down my crack and dipped between my legs to find me wet, overflowing. "Oh, fuck, baby. You liked that, didn't you?"

Her fingers plunged into my cunt and she pumped them in and out, fast and hard. My pussy was making hungry slurping noises around her fingers and she added another one. I was open and sucking her into me. She fucked me harder and murmured encouragement as I fucked back at her and tried to take her hand.

"I missed this pussy so much when I was gone," she murmured. "Did you miss my fist, baby?"

I was moaning and fucking myself onto her four fingers. It occurred to me that she needed this as much as I did, that she had her own frustrations built up in her body that could only be released in violence, that had to be taken out on my ass and in my pussy.

"Tell me how bad you want my fist," she said, her fingers pumping into me. "Tell me how much you want my hand inside your pussy."

I felt like I could never be full enough. I felt like I wanted both her fists inside me buried up to her forearm. All I could say was, "Fuck me, fuck me, fuck me."

Abruptly, Bren pulled her fingers from my cunt and a sob burst from my throat. She slapped her hand down on my ass where the skin would be black and blue tomorrow. I realized my mistake, and through wracking sobs I tried to rectify it. "Please, Sir, please fuck me?"

"Too little, too late. Come on, you can do better than that."

"Please, Sir," I didn't know if my words were intelligible through my tears; all I knew was that I needed her fist inside me and I'd babble anything to get it. "Please, Sir, I want your fist inside me so bad. Please, baby, please, Bren? You know how much I love your hand inside me, you know you make me come so hard. I love you, baby, I love the way you fuck me. I need to come with you inside me. Please make me come, please Daddy? I need your fist so bad, I need my daddy's fist inside me." I broke off, sobbing so hard I couldn't talk. I barely knew what I was saying, who I was saying it to. Maybe I thought if I appealed to the multiplicity of who my lover was to me I would make my need known. There was something horrible and divine about being made to beg for what I wanted. My heart swelled along with my clit at the mix of shame and total surrender to love that it produced inside my body.

"Tell me how much you need it."

I was shaking, choking on my tears. "I think I'll die if you don't fuck me, I need you so bad."

She laughed, standing there behind me, and some small animal part of me froze, recognizing a meanness in her that startled me.

"Poor little slut, I doubt it's that bad." She ran her fingers over my welts, hard enough to make me shy away from her.

"You'll have to prove it. You want me to fuck you, you'll have to work for it. Convince me."

Her hand was on the back of my neck, her fingers twining in my hair. Time felt strange, slowed down, then sped up, as she wrenched my head back and pulled me off the bed. I had one of those weird out-of-body perspectives, seeing myself shaking and crying, makeup smeared all over my face, staring wild eyed up at her from my sudden position on the floor. The vantage point made her look taller.

She looked down at me in a heap at her feet, disheveled, snot running down my face, and sighed. "We can't have this," she said as she roughly squeezed my nose, wiping the mucus from my face and tossing it on the floor.

I started bawling harder and she looked at me with disgust. "Look at you crying in a heap on the floor." She nudged me with her boot. "I know I train my sluts better than that."

I was broken down into warring factions. There were parts that wanted to cry myself into oblivion, parts that wanted to beg for the privilege of licking her boots for hours and a sudden rebellion that was all for leaping up and decking her. Submission has always been a mixed bag for me.

I chose the path of least resistance and arranged myself with my sore ass perched on my heels and my wrists together behind my arched back. I kept my eyes downcast, not only to complete the submissive picture, but also to hide the spark of defiance I knew was clearly visible.

"Much better," she said, stepping forward until my forehead rested on the rough denim of her crotch. The pulse quickened between my thighs and I moaned at being so close to her. Something in me softened and I quit fighting myself, gave up any notion of fighting her.

Her fingers tangled themselves into my hair and she pulled

my head back. "Are you ready to prove it, baby? Prove how much you want my fist?" Her voice was low and sweet, a disorienting contrast to the pain building in my scalp. "I'll make it easy on you. Just nod your head."

It wasn't easy, of course. She was holding my hair so close to the scalp that the motion was barely possible, but I did the best I could.

"Good girl," she purred and with her free hand, pulled down her zipper. I moaned and tried to lower my head to see what she was uncovering, but she held my head firm, forcing eye contact. "Listen, bitch, here's the deal. You are going to suck my cunt like you want me to fuck your pussy. Satisfy me and I'll take care of you. Understood?"

She released her hold on my hair and I nodded, feeling the tears drying on my face. "Yes, please," I said, feeling calm for the first time in days.

She smiled down at me and pushed her jeans and briefs off her hips. "Pull these down for me, will you?"

I was quick to oblige and groaned as the smell of her hit me. Her hands cupped my head and I got a quick view of her glistening thighs and swollen clit as she guided my mouth onto her.

It was all pretense, all a game. She knew I would lick her to orgasm anytime, anywhere. It was something I begged for, drooled for, a service I would perform at the slightest hint that she wanted me. The mind fuck was for her more than me, the psychological domination broken into the right code words to navigate the traps in her head, make it safe for her to drop her pants. But I would be lying if I said it didn't make me hot as fuck, if I denied the aching pulse in my clit as she pulled my face into her cunt and rocked herself back and forth between my lips, running the show. Nothing is ever simple; it's never only what it is on the face of the thing. Our insides were spread wide inside a room of mirrors, reflecting ourselves back to each other over and over, a writhing mass of pink and red organs.

I moaned into her cunt, vibrating sound off her clit. She was breathing heavily above me, groaning deep in her throat as she pulled my face into her. I lapped at the shaft of her clit, first avoiding the sensitive head, circling around it, then sucked it into my mouth and licked her with fast stokes, using the very point of my tongue.

Her hands tightened on my head and her hips stilled, holding me exactly where she wanted me. I felt the tension building in her abdomen, felt her muscles quiver and begin to shake. A moan starting deep in the pit of her stomach escaped her as her hips jerked forward against my mouth. I increased the pressure of my lips around her clit, pressed her hard with the flat of my tongue, felt her gush down my chin as she came in my mouth. Her body lurched forward and she bent over as the contractions rolled through her.

As she relaxed I kissed her, nuzzled her pubic hair, ran my hands over her shaky thighs. She straightened her body and took a deep breath, gently pulled my face away from her cunt and looked down at me. "I love you so fucking much," she said, and I knew she was Bren now, just Bren, and I was just me, her girl.

She pulled me up and led me over to the bed, stripping me of my clothing as we went. Gently, she pushed me back onto the loft. The sheets felt surprisingly cool against the heat of my newly beaten skin. I spread my legs wide for her, showing her how wet I was for her. The time for begging had passed, but I looked up at my love's face and said, "Please, baby? I want you to fuck me so bad."

She crawled up on the bed with me. I tugged at her shirt and gave her a pleading look. She pulled the shirt over her head and threw it on the floor. I ran my hands over her bound chest and tugged at the fastenings, unwrapped her like the only present I had ever wanted. She kissed my lips softly, slipping her tongue into my mouth, her hand trailing my jaw, pulling me toward her. Her other hand went between my spread thighs and her fingers pressed at my opening.

My blood pressure spiked and I groaned through gritted teeth, "Yes, please, baby, please fuck me, please."

She grinned down at me and thrust three fingers inside my pussy, pumping me hard, no longer making me wait. She felt so fucking good, and I told her so. I thrust my hips, raised them up off the bed to meet her hand, and she added another finger. I felt full and like I would never be full, never have enough of her inside me.

She held her mouth right above mine, breathing my breath, breathing my moans and whimpers, running her tongue along my lips. "More, baby, please, more, I want all of you," I said into her mouth.

I felt the muscles at the mouth of my cunt burn as she added her thumb and pushed her knuckles against my opening. Maybe my pussy was bigger in my mind. Maybe the juice gushing from my cunt was too watery for such intense penetration. Maybe I didn't give a fuck about any of the obstacles; I was going to take that big fucking hand of hers up into my pussy if I tore myself doing it.

She rotated her hand, twisting, rubbing her knuckles all around my opening. I felt like I was about to black out or fly away or forget my own name.

On cue, like she had read my mind, Bren started chanting my name, told me to give it to her. She coaxed, calling me *sweetheart, sugar, darling*. She demanded, calling me *bitch, slut, whore*. She said my name and my cunt opened up and she slid her fist inside me.

She rocked her fist, rotated it, making me twitch and moan. I clenched my muscles around her wrist, drawing her in. She groaned deep in her throat and pumped her fist against the resistance of my tightened opening. My world narrowed to a sensation of pressure so deep and wide, pleasure and pain held in an open palm, related but separate enough to be different. My cunt was full of bittersweet and with one right move I would explode.

Bren made it. She rocked her fist upward, her knuckles kneading into the spongy tissue on the roof of my pussy, and it set me off like a firecracker. Shock waves spread out from my cunt through my body making me shake and spasm. Her rocking fist kept me anchored, grounding me in the intense sensations of my body. She fucked me through my come until it got to be too much, and I squeezed her hard with my muscles and begged her to stop.

I opened my eyes, not knowing I had closed them. It was dark in my room and I was drenched in sweat, drenched in come, dizzy and high from the fuck. An early night breeze was coming through the open window, sweet relief swirling through the thick heat of the air. Bren's skin was sticking to mine everywhere that we touched and she was quiet beside me, her hand playing with my hair.

"I missed you, angel," she said and kissed my sweaty cheek.

LOVERS' MOON

Ren Peters

Mickey looked up from her book and watched as the sun dipped closer and closer to the horizon. The beach was almost empty of people, and she was feeling a little lonely, but there she sat...waiting. She'd expected it, though. Every time anyone showed the slightest interest at all in that car, Reggie had to take them out for a spin. She was like a kid with a new toy. What was she thinking? Reggie *was* a kid with a new toy. And what a toy! Mickey had to admit there was something very sexy about it. Maybe it was the speed and the vibration of the engine you could actually feel through the seat. Thinking of that vibration and of Reggie, Mickey shifted uncomfortably in her beach chair. *Where* is *that girl?*

"Hey there." Reggie slipped out of her sandals and dropped down cross-legged on the blanket next to the beach chair.

Mickey closed the book in her lap and turned to look at her lover. "Hey, you. Where's Cindy?"

"She'll be along. I dropped her off at her car so she can move it closer. Most of the front row is empty where I parked. I hope you don't mind, I told her we'd help her schlep the stuff from the beach."

"No, not at all. Good idea. I missed you." Mickey blew a kiss in Reggie's direction and got a raised eyebrow in reply.

"Careful there," Reggie warned quietly.

"What?"

"You know what." Reggie smiled at her partner who returned a silly grin.

"I want to go home and...you-know-what," Mickey murmured, as she ran her tongue seductively over her upper lip and waggled her eyebrows.

"Stop it!" Reggie hissed. "Jesus! You're worse than a kid!" All day, Mickey had been flirting with her, but they were with a straight friend who worked with them and they weren't out at work. "Just behave. We'll leave soon." Reggie paused and looked out over the ocean at the last rays of the sunset, then gestured toward the horizon. "I guess I missed a good show, huh?"

"It was pretty...but it would've been better with you here. So how was the ride? She enjoy it?"

A chuckle burst from Reggie's lips. "That's an understatement! But I'll let you enjoy her telling it. I think she was a little afraid at first, but that didn't last. Ah! Here she comes."

Mickey sat forward and waved to Cindy as she trudged to their blankets. "What took you so long? Did the ride tire you out?"

"Oh, no! It was invigorating. I never thought a car could be that much fun. It was a real disappointment to drive my old clunker after that."

"So where'd she take you?"

Cindy's face brightened, and she became instantly animated.

"Well, the main roads were jammed with beach traffic, so we took the back road through the village. Everybody looked at us as we passed. That was fun. But we had to go slow. On the way back, though, the escape road was empty, and speed demon here went over seventy-five miles an hour. I even saw the spoiler come up! So close to the ground, the speed's a little scary, but it's exciting too. It's amazing how you can really feel like you're part of a car. I loved it!"

"Uh-oh, Reg, looks like another Porsche convert." Mickey laughed and stood. "C'mon, let's get this stuff back to Cindy's car so we can be on our way."

Reggie gathered up the beach chairs while Cindy and Mickey shook out and folded the blankets. Then the three women made the short walk to the parking lot. After loading everything into Cindy's car, they stood beside the Porsche. As Reggie opened the driver's-side door, Cindy said, "I still can't believe you bought this."

"I can't either." Reggie laughed.

The soft light of dusk caressed the cream-white Boxster. Its curvaceous styling was classic Porsche—low, wide and not a straight line anywhere. The interior was in contrasting black with soft, rich leather seats. Reggie lightly stroked the bumper. "It's been a dream of mine for so long. Maybe buying it now was a midlife crisis thing…turning fifty and all…but I've wanted a Porsche ever since I started driving. It may be a used car, but it's an incredible machine."

"Uh…excuse me!" Mickey wagged her finger at Reggie. "As I've been repeatedly told, when speaking of Porsches, the proper term is 'certified previously owned vee-hick-ull.' Apparently they have standards to maintain."

Laughing, Cindy said, "Well, whatever it is, it's gorgeous. And thank you for giving me a ride in it. It was—how can I put it?—almost orgasmic!"

That brought laughter from all three.

"C'mon, chief, let's go." Mickey was already in her seat with her seat belt fastened.

Reggie slipped behind the wheel and reached for her seat belt. "Do you want to leave the top down?" she asked, hoping for a yes.

"Of course! It's a full moon tonight. I wanna howl all the way home."

"You're in rare form, m'dear," Reggie said as she pulled away from the curb. They gave a wave as they passed their friend and drove out of the parking lot.

Mickey drew her shoulder-length auburn hair into a pony-tail, then settled in the seat that snugly held her small athletic body. Her five feet two inches had ample room in the Porsche's cockpit interior. Luxuriating in the space, she stretched her legs. She felt comfortable and wanted their day at the shore to last a bit longer. "Hey, let's not go home on the highway. Let's go by way of the lighthouse and then drive up the shore road until we run out of ocean and have to head west."

"You sure?"

"Yeah. It's a gorgeous night and I love driving with my baby in her Porsche with the top down."

"Ahh, so it's not me, but the car you love."

"No. You first, hon. It's always been you first." Mickey rested her hand on her lover's thigh. Reggie sighed at the touch as she turned onto Ocean Road.

Reggie couldn't quite understand why, but she had needed this car. It made her feel strong and in control. Cindy's comment that the ride was almost orgasmic had surprised her because that's exactly the feeling she had every time she drove it. The speed, the instant power, the way it hugged the road and caressed the curves—she felt it all in the very core of her being. She knew it seemed silly, but when she drove the Porsche, she was at one with the car; she was a power ready to be released. The pulsating throb of the engine at her back brought a rush of adrenalin each time she floored the accelerator, and she loved to drive it wickedly fast. It was a damned aphrodisiac! When she washed the Porsche, she swore it was like making love to a woman. The feel of the sudsy cloth gliding smoothly over the undulating contours was positively arousing. She shivered at the thought.

"You're not cold, are you?" Mickey turned to look at Reggie.

Sitting erect in her seat, her short dark hair ruffling lightly in the breeze, Reggie's long, lithe body was perfectly at ease behind the wheel. Mickey looked lovingly at her finely chiseled profile, the Roman nose and high cheekbones above full and sensuous lips. She thought how much she truly adored her.

"Nah. Not at all. I was just thinking about something. It got me all goosey." Reggie smiled sheepishly.

"So. Are you going to share?" Mickey wasn't going to let her shy partner get away with that bit of innuendo.

"You'll think I'm silly. And you'll laugh."

"No, I won't. I promise. And if I do, I'll hide it really, really well. Honest." Mickey giggled.

"I know you're going to laugh," Reggie said, "but I know you won't let me enjoy this ride unless I tell you. So here goes..." She paused. "Driving this car is a real turn-on for me."

"Yeah, I know. I like riding in it, too."

"No, no. It's more than just liking it. It really turns me on. It's arousing. I feel like I'm part of the car. I feel its strength, its surges of power. I feel the road, the steady throb of the engine. I feel it right in my...you know." Reggie hesitated, and her face turned crimson. "It's like Cindy said. It's almost...orgasmic."

Her earnest voice seemed to plead for understanding. Then she added quietly, "Except, for me, it's closer than just almost."

"Why, Regina Maria Rizzo, I'm speechless. This car really has had an effect on you." Mickey leaned back in her seat and quietly watched the road ahead.

They were silent for a few minutes. Then the curve of the road brought them into view of the rising moon trailing its light across the ocean. Full and low in the sky, it seemed almost close enough to touch. It was stunning, and Reggie drew in a quick, sharp breath at the sight of it.

"It's a lovers' moon, hon," Mickey murmured, rubbing her hand up and down Reggie's thigh. "I'm glad we're driving home the long way."

"Me too." Reggie gave Mickey's hand a squeeze. "I love you so much." She smiled at Mickey then turned her attention back to the road.

In quiet comfort, they drove the winding miles that hugged the shoreline. Reggie never moved the car out of third gear as they meandered past beaches and beach homes until they came to the highway that turned west toward their home. Earlier in the day, this section of road would have been crammed bumper-to-bumper with beachgoers returning to the city. At this time of night, however, it was almost deserted and Reggie was eager to let the Porsche fly.

"It's safe here for a little speed. How's about we live on the wild side for a few miles?"

At Mickey's nod, Reggie accelerated and quickly moved the Porsche through fourth and into fifth gear. The spoiler deployed at seventy-five miles an hour, and Reggie let the speedometer climb to eighty before leveling off. The throaty purr of the engine and the gentle vibration of the car against the road were palpable.

Excitement in her eyes, Reggie yelled into the wind, "I—love—this—car!" They sped along, moon at their backs, the empty road before them glistening in its silver light. Reggie was excited and happy, feeling the power, feeling the road with her lover beside her. "Do you feel it, Mickey? Do you feel the power?"

Moving her hand from Reggie's thigh to between her legs, Mickey grinned and said, "Oh, yeah, I *feel* it. I *definitely* feel it."

"Don't do that!" Reggie squirmed in her seat. "I'm on the edge here anyway. I don't need any encouragement."

Mickey's hand stilled for a moment, then she turned in her seat toward Reggie. "Just keep your hands on the wheel...and your eyes on the road. I have some business to take care of." With that, she deftly unbuttoned and unzipped Reggie's cargo shorts. "I love my girl in her little butch shorts."

"Hey. What are you doing? We're on a public road and, if you hadn't noticed, the top is down!"

"Stop talking and don't worry. You're going way too fast for anyone to see anything."

With that, Mickey tugged Reggie's shorts down a bit and slipped her hand into the soft warmth they covered.

"Mmm," groaned Reggie. "You're going to kill me. And I just might kill us!"

"Oooh, you weren't kidding when you said this car turns you on! I'm a bit jealous. I can see I'm going to have to do something special to win you back."

Mickey undid her seat belt, maneuvered herself onto her knees and leaned over the center console. "Damn. These Boxsters weren't designed for sex. Lift up your rear end so I can get some leverage." After Reggie unbuckled her seat belt and lifted up off the seat, Mickey slipped her left arm under Reggie and pulled her shorts down a little more. "You just keep driving, baby, just keep driving." With that, she licked her way up Reggie's inner thigh to her center.

Straight-armed and stiff-legged, Reggie shuddered as the car went a little faster.

"Oh, you are so ready for me," Mickey breathed. Her tongue made swirls around Reggie's softness then slowly dipped in and out of her.

Shivering, Reggie moaned softly as the car went faster still. "I'm so close and we're going way too fast," she gasped.

"It's all right, love, just a moment more," Mickey whispered before finding and sucking the swollen bud for all she was worth.

Reggie's hips rose higher. She was standing on her left foot, trying not to press down any farther on the gas pedal, but the car continued to gather speed. "Oh, shit, I'm coming!" Fiercely gripping the steering wheel, she pulled herself up even farther while the shudders ran through her. As the spasms subsided, Mickey quickly pulled away, sat back and rebuckled her seat belt.

"Hold on to that wheel, sweetheart; there's an eighteen-wheeler trailing us on the left, and you're doing more than ninety."

As Reggie collapsed against her seat, her right foot slipped off the gas pedal and their speed slowly clocked down: ninety... eighty...seventy. The truck barreled past them and they were alone again on the road. Reggie's glazed eyes stared ahead. She wasn't seeing much, but she was feeling everything. Her whole body was alive, pulsing with the rhythm of the tires, the vibration in the steering wheel, the thrum of the engine, all resonating in the aching throb between her legs.

"Touch me," she barely whispered. "Please."

Mickey reached out to put her hand on Reggie's thigh, but Reggie took the hand and pressed it between her legs. "Please, hold me here. I need you here."

Seventy…sixty…fifty…the spoiler retracted and they continued to coast in silence, straight into the dark ahead. Mickey could feel Reggie pulsing against the heel of her hand. At forty miles an hour, Reggie pushed down hard on the accelerator and on Mickey's hand. Mickey automatically began a rhythmic kneading as the Porsche surged ahead: fifty-five…sixty-five… seventy-five. The spoiler deployed once again as the car raced on. The burst of speed and the pressure of her lover's hand brought another wave of climax shuddering through Reggie's body and once more she collapsed into her seat and let the car coast.

"Oh, my," Reggie sighed. "This is quite a ride." She looked over at Mickey with a weak smile. "I think I need to pull over for a minute and…uh…get myself together."

"Whatever you need, Reg. I love you so very much." Mickey smiled back and withdrew her hand.

Reggie slowed down and maneuvered the car into the breakdown lane. When they came to a full stop, she pulled up and zipped her shorts. Turning, she unbuckled Mickey's seat belt, pulled her toward her, and rested her forehead on Mickey's shoulder.

"You make my fantasies come true…even if I haven't thought of them yet. I adore you."

Mickey pulled back and looked at Reggie. "You're *my* fantasy, sweetie. You always have been."

Their lips touched in the gentle knowing caress of longtime lovers. Then, with a twinkle in her eye, Reggie asked, "Hey! You wanna drive now?"

Mickey quickly reached for the door handle. "Hell, yes! If you think *you* were ready…"

As they laughingly changed places, Reggie looked back at the moon. "You were right, Mick—it really is a lovers' moon."

THE OFFICE GRIND

R. G. Emanuelle

Nina entered the Lotus Flower Lounge tense and irritated. She beelined for a small cocktail table and flopped into one of the chairs, slammed her purse down, ordered a cosmopolitan from the waitress and took a few deep breaths to relax herself. Clicking her nails on the table, she huffed with impatience, and when her drink finally arrived, she almost grabbed it out of the server's hands.

Halfway through her drink, Nina was still on edge. She moved to the bar for more immediate service and something stronger than a cosmo, something that wouldn't pussyfoot around.

It was one o'clock and the lounge was empty save for Nina, a couple at another table and a woman at the other end of the bar. Nina was paying attention to only the rose-colored concoction in front of her, but her blood began to heat when she scanned the lounge and realized that the woman at the bar was watching her.

From the corner of her eye, Nina saw dark hair but she

couldn't get a further sense of what the stranger looked like. She dared not turn around and give the impression that she was interested, but she kept an eye on the other woman peripherally.

The woman watched intently as Nina knocked back the remaining sweet-sour liquid and ordered a dry vodka martini. When it arrived, she forcefully pulled the olives off the toothpick with her teeth.

"Don't bite down so hard on those toothpicks. They'll ruin your teeth," the woman said from two seats over, flashing a seductive smile.

When did she move over? Nina debated responding as she chewed her olives.

"Tough day?"

Nina decided to ignore the stranger, who was intruding on her private moment of pissiness. Couldn't a woman go into a bar for a drink without being hit on? She wasn't looking for companionship, just a postlunch belt. She was too stressed out to be nice to anyone, too tightly wound to entertain the notion of flirting and seducing—or of being seduced. But the confident grin on the other woman's face was quickly melting Nina's resistance.

"Oh, just meetings." Nina sighed. "They're driving me crazy. I feel more and more like they're taking place just to provide the *team* with an opportunity to stroke each other's egos." She loaded sarcasm on the word *team*. "They're a bunch of smarmy, college-boy schmucks who only know what they've been taught and nothing more. My boss—Pompous Windbag, as I like to call him—is an egoist whose only interest is pawning off responsibility so he can go play golf."

"Wow. That sounds terrible," the stranger said with a hint of sympathy, as she moved to the bar stool right next to Nina and stuck out her hand. "I'm Casey, by the way." Her short hair was pushed back greaser style, exposing the planes of her smooth face. She had startling green eyes that Nina was sure had caused many a woman's panties to mysteriously fall off.

Nina blushed, thinking how spoiled she must sound blurting out her office woes to a complete stranger. *A handsome, beautiful stranger.* She shook Casey's hand and it was warm in hers, shooting a hot wave up her arm down into her stomach...then lower still. It was as if a force field around Casey had expanded to include Nina. Her pulse sped up several beats. "I'm Nina," she managed, quickly releasing Casey's hand. *What the hell?*

She checked her watch and nearly jumped. She'd been AWOL from the office for three hours. But if Pompous Windbag could schedule a meeting at five o'clock, then she could take an extralong lunch. "I'm so sorry," she said. "I'm sure you didn't want to hear all that."

"No problem." Casey motioned to the bartender. "Hey, Luanne, another beer for me and another martini for the lady." Luanne smiled at Casey and turned to get the vodka from the back bar. As Casey put in the order, Nina surreptitiously studied her. Casey's black, short-sleeved shirt showed off her well-toned arms, even calling attention to the vein than ran down each bicep, just barely above the plane of her muscles. *Yum.* Nina wanted to run her tongue along the edge of the black tattoo that peeked out from the bottom of Casey's sleeve.

The bartender put Nina's drink in front of her and poured a beer for Casey while throwing her what Nina could only pin as a "knowing" look. Evidently Luanne knew Casey, but did she know something about her that Nina should know?

Casey picked her glass up and tipped it toward Nina. "Cheers."

Reluctantly, Nina lifted her martini in response. "Cheers." As she sipped, she quickly considered her situation. Yes, she *was* too wound up. She mentally boxed up her reservations about Casey and put them in the back of the closet. Taking a deep breath, she allowed the alcohol to invade her bloodstream, to relax her muscles—to release her inhibitions. Almost involuntarily, she squeezed her thighs together.

Casey's gem green eyes bore deeply into hers as if seeking information, perhaps permission. "So, what do you do for fun?" Casey asked, flashing that smile again.

Nina felt a throbbing between her legs that would be eased in only one way. She turned so that their knees touched, sending electric currents up her thighs. *To hell with it.* "I enjoy reading, listening to music, going to the theater," Nina said, running her hand up Casey's tight forearm. Moving her face very close to Casey's, she whispered, "And fucking." *Did I really just say that?* Never had she been so forward—not in a bar, anyway.

Casey's eyes had been dancing playfully over Nina's face, neck and the curves of her breasts, but they were now steady and serious. The intensity of her gaze was almost frightening. Nina shivered at the thought of what this woman could do to her.

Casey's skin visibly prickled as she slipped her arm out from Nina's caresses and brought it down to her lap. "I think that's a healthy pursuit," she said, her voice deepening to a low, sultry tone. Her fingertips slipped under the hem of Nina's skirt.

Nina wanted Casey to take her into the bathroom, throw her against the wall and fuck her right then and there. She exhaled sharply when Casey removed her hand from Nina's leg and lifted it back up to the bar. Along the way, she brushed Nina's nipple, barely, almost imperceptibly, driving her wild. She knew where she stood.

"How's that beer?" Nina asked, licking her lips before she sipped her martini.

Casey looked at her glass quizzically. There was about an

inch of liquid left. She tilted her head sideways and lifted one corner of her mouth in a coy smile. "It's just fine. Why do you ask?"

"Because as soon as you're done with it, I thought we could go somewhere and...talk."

Casey regarded her for a moment, then picked up her glass and downed its remnants. Without a word, Nina got up and Casey followed her out the door.

Casey marveled at the enormity of Nina's office. "Wow," she said. "I don't think the War Room at the Pentagon is this big." She bounced her hand over the top of each chair that surrounded a long conference table that was perpendicular to Nina's desk.

"It's good to be V.P.," Nina said with mock arrogance. Throwing her purse on the desk, she followed Casey with a lustful gaze. *God, she's unbelievably sexy.* What was she thinking bringing this woman back here? She watched Casey move, watched the way her ass looked in her black jeans. *Hot sex with a woman I just picked up in a bar, that's what.* Hot, sweaty sex in her office, where she sat day after day, reviewing boring reports, balancing budgets and putting up with a pack of smug men who thought nothing of ogling her breasts when she spoke. Well, those pricks only wished for what she was about to give Casey.

When Casey had circled the entire conference table and thumped the last chair, she stepped over to Nina and brushed the hair off her shoulder. Leaning in toward her, Casey kept her eyes locked on Nina's. Accustomed to being in control, Nina instead felt herself being willed into submission. Their lips met, softly at first, playing and teasing, causing Nina's breath to come harder and sharper.

Casey slowly ran her tongue across Nina's lips. Nina's panting increased, but otherwise she stood motionless, lips parted, eyes riveted to Casey's face. Those green eyes sent chills up her spine and when Casey's lips pressed down hard, Nina's entire head tingled. This woman was electric.

The quivering in Casey's arms made Nina smile. It meant that Casey was just as turned on as she was. The aching in every inch of her body was weakening Nina, and she was so wet that all Casey would have to do was place one finger on her and Nina was sure she'd explode. *Just rip my clothes off and ravish me.*

But Casey seemed to have other ideas. She was going nice and slow, and the grin on her face was saying, "Patience has its rewards."

When Casey pressed her lips firmly on Nina's and one tongue found the other, Casey finally closed her eyes. She pulled Nina against her and moved her hands up Nina's ass, across her waist and over her breasts, catching the nipples in the crease between thumb and forefinger. "God, you are so fucking hot," she growled. Nina moaned and ran her hands up Casey's arms, squeezing her shoulders, reveling in how solid they felt, how strong.

She knew she turned heads, knew that people thought she was hot with her long, auburn hair and dark chocolate eyes. They'd told her so. And she dressed the part, too. The jacket of her expensive tailored suit stopped at her round hips and the skirt was short enough to show her smooth, curvy legs—one of her best features, she'd always thought—which were accentuated by a pair of black pumps that said, "I'm a busy executive but come fuck me anyway." She knew all that. But something about the way Casey looked at her made her feel sexy beyond the clothes she was wearing, beyond the shape of her body.

They unbuttoned each other's shirts, and Nina shoved her thigh between Casey's. They began to grind, nice and hard. Nina's jacket slipped off her shoulders and hung at her elbows.

When Casey had undone three of Nina's buttons, she unlocked her lips from Nina's mouth and dropped down to her breast, simultaneously pulling her bra cups down just low enough to expose her nipples. Gently, Casey pushed her face against Nina's skin. Nina inhaled sharply, and her breasts heaved upward. She placed a hand on the back of Casey's head to keep her there.

"You're gorgeous," Casey said between kisses. She traced the curves of Nina's breasts with her tongue while her fingers squeezed Nina's nipples. They hardened, and Nina groaned. When Casey's mouth reached one erect nipple, she circled it with her tongue and then pulled on it with her lips before gently biting it. Nina gasped, air hissing between her teeth.

Nina's underwear was soaked—she hadn't thought she could get this wet—as she rubbed her pussy against Casey's hard thigh. She was just sliding her hand into Casey's pants when male voices sounded from the hallway, loud enough to be heard through the heavy wooden door and getting louder by the second.

"Holy shit!" Nina froze. "Get under the desk now," she commanded, pushing Casey down. Casey hit the floor and crawled beneath the dark wooden desk. Quickly, Nina fixed her bra, buttoned her blouse, and straightened her jacket just before her coworkers walked in. *Damn it, don't these bastards know how to knock?*

"Nina," her boss said, as if he was surprised to see her. "You're here. Good. We have to move the meeting. There's some kind of leak in the conference room. You don't mind if we meet in here, do you?"

Nina stared at him. *Was it 5:00 already? Damn!* Nina didn't think he cared if she minded or not. "Uh, no. That's fine. Um, if you don't mind, I'll just sit at my desk rather than at the conference table." She cleared her throat and sat down, pulling her chair in close. *Thank god this desk has solid sides.*

"You okay? You're sweating," Arrogant Fucker, one of Nina's subordinates, noted. She thought of him that way because he was the kind of guy who thought himself an expert in everything.

If you only knew. Nina wiped her temples. "It's hot in here." Smiling nervously, she shrugged and he turned to find a seat at the table.

Jerry, the boss's favorite ass-kisser, set the screen up. Arrogant Fucker turned the lights off and drew the shades, and the room was plunged into darkness. Someone began a PowerPoint slideshow on a laptop. Men were talking, pointing at the progressing slides, but all Nina could think about was Casey under the desk. *Jesus Christ. How the fuck do I get out of this?* There was no way she could sneak Casey out now. The laptop exuded enough light that she'd be seen. *Fuck.*

As if in response to her thoughts, Nina felt her skirt being pushed up. Alarmed at first, she carefully reached under the desk to put a stop to Casey's hands. No, this couldn't happen.

Casey's fingers again slid up Nina's thighs, beneath her skirt, then back down toward her knees. Then they moved slowly up the inside of Nina's thighs. They soon found Nina's panties and tugged at them.

Holy fuck. Nina swallowed, not sure she could handle this.

Somebody was muttering something that Nina didn't catch. She didn't know who was speaking, but she didn't care. The fear she'd felt a moment ago was giving way to excitement. There was something deliciously subversive about sitting in a room full of men with a woman under her desk teasing her.

She bit her lip and slowly lifted one cheek and then the other, allowing Casey to pull her underwear down her thighs, past her calves and over her come-fuck-me shoes. As if they had minds of their own, Nina's knees parted and she felt Casey's head between them, her hair tickling. Casey first kissed the flesh on each thigh, then began nibbling as she got closer and closer to the top. Nina swore she could feel the smile on Casey's lips against her skin.

"We'll show 'em who's boss, right Nina?" Arrogant Fucker said. *I'll show you who's boss. When was the last time* you *had a woman between your legs, you fucker?* She nodded in assent, bit her lip to prevent herself from groaning and hoped her face wasn't betraying the anticipation building between her legs.

Casey started where Nina's ass met the leather chair. She slid the tip of her tongue up, up, up—dipping briefly into Nina's hot wetness—until it glided just past her clit, making wide, slow circles. Nina grabbed the rubber stress ball on her desk and squeezed it hard, trying to maintain composure.

A red laser dot hit a spot on the presentation and Nina's boss said, "Nina, how do you feel about this segment?" In the glow from the PowerPoint, Arrogant Fucker glanced at her, puzzled. She trained her gaze on the screen as Casey kissed her pussy, then slipped her tongue inside until Nina felt firm lips against her. *Oh, god...*

Nina arched her back just a bit, as if she were merely readjusting her position in her chair. She opened her legs wider. "Uh, I think we've successfully penetrated that market." She kept her breathing slow and easy, though she was struggling. Casey pulled her tongue out and licked Nina as if she were a melting ice-cream cone. Nina bit her lip again.

Casey circled again around Nina's clit with her tongue, but Nina felt her change position under the desk and she gripped the stress ball so hard that her fingers burned. Casey was exploring her pussy with her fingers, moistening them, until she slowly slid them in. Out. In. Slowly. Then, increasing pressure on Nina's swollen clit, she began thrusting her fingers in and out faster as Nina's pussy opened wider and grew wetter and smoother.

Casey's lips completely covered Nina's clit and she stopped

licking every now and then to suck gently on it. *Sweet Jesus.* Nothing had felt that good in a long, long time. She wanted to scream out that she was getting fucked right here in her office, right in front of all these full-of-shit guys. She felt a third finger enter, filling her in an exquisite way. A low "Ah," escaped her lips.

"What's that, Nina?" Pompous Windbag asked.

Nina forced herself to open her eyes. Several people were looking at her. "I said, 'Ah.' I didn't see *that* coming." Shit. Was she making sense? Apparently so, because some of them nodded in agreement and they all turned back to the screen.

Nina closed her eyes again. She could feel Casey's cheeks, slick with her juices, rubbing against her thighs. *Jesus Christ, she's been around this block before.* Nina clamped her thighs around Casey's head, but realizing that Casey might not be able to breathe, she opened wide again, allowing Casey to lick in wider strokes, strokes that sent tide after tide of ecstasy down Nina's thighs. *Oh. God.*

Casey's hand slipped underneath Nina's leg and wrapped around her thigh, pulling the executive harder against her mouth. Casey's hand roamed up Nina's hip and grabbed on to the little extra flesh that cushioned her pelvic area. Where Casey's fingers pressed, little bonfires erupted. Nina willed herself not to moan, clamping her jaws together as hard as she could. She replaced the stress ball on the desk and raked the fingers of that hand through Casey's silky hair while her other hand gripped the arm of her chair. Her knuckles strained from the pressure.

She kept running her hand through Casey's hair, lightly at first, then grasped it tightly, bringing Casey's face harder against her pussy. Casey increased the speed of her licking and the pounding of her fingers into Nina. *Fuck, yeah. Every meeting should be like this.*

A familiar tension built up in Nina's pussy right beneath

Casey's tongue, and her muscles tightened around Casey's fingers. *Oh, yeah. A little more...* An explosion started in her clit that rippled up inside her, through her stomach and chest until it reached her throat. She kept her mouth closed, straining against her urge to scream. She glanced around the table furtively to see if anyone had noticed anything—they were all caught up in their stupid project. Closing her eyes again, she convulsed silently. *Oh, my god...* She exhaled as quietly as she dared and when her body stopped trembling, she opened her eyes. The team was oblivious. Completely. She'd just gotten fucked not ten feet from them and nobody knew. As she sagged back into her chair, the presentation ended and someone turned the lights on. She sat up straighter.

"Nina, you've been quiet," Pompous Windbag said, turning to her. "What are your thoughts?"

Nina took a couple of seconds to let the sex-induced fog roll away from her brain. "Well, given what I've seen here, I think more research is in order before we insert ourselves in that market."

Pompous Windbag nodded once, seemingly satisfied with that answer, and announced their next meeting date. As the team filed out, he turned to her. "You *are* sweating. Are you sure you're all right?"

"Definitely. Very. Just a little tired."

"That's my girl." He tossed a wave at her and exited. Nina stood up and pushed her skirt back down so she could close the door. This time, she locked it.

Casey emerged from underneath the desk and wiped Nina's juice from her chin, a sly smile spreading across her face.

Stunned and sated, Nina leaned against the door, her hand on the doorknob for support. Then she grinned an evil, naughty little grin. It was the V.P.'s turn to have some fun.

NOT AFRAID TO GET HER HANDS DIRTY

Teresa Noelle Roberts

A llie, this is Lucia Chen. I corralled her into helping with the sofa." When my friend Nate, who had the downstairs of the duplex, said he'd borrow a truck from his sometime-lover Ben to pick up my new couch, I figured he'd borrow Ben, too. Lucia didn't look as likely a sofa-mover as Ben, but she was definitely hotter to me, even if my view of her was a little blurry thanks to the pain medication I was on. She had short, wavy, almost black hair; full lips accented with red lipstick; a compact but strong-looking figure and an exotic-but-I-can't-quite-place-it look that made sense with a name like Lucia Chen. She wavered in and out of focus a bit, but what I could see, I liked.

"Thanks so much. Picking the damn thing up and saving delivery charges seemed like a great idea until two days ago." Which was when I'd slipped in slush, broken my right arm and screwed up the left wrist and elbow, which were now Ace-bandaged to remind me to move them as little as I could manage.

"Glad to help out. If you're going to be whacked on pain meds for a few more days, you might as well do it on a comfy couch." Have I mentioned that the day I fell was trash day, and Nate and I had muscled the broken-springed old couch out to the curb the night before? Hence the scramble to get the new one.

Out of instinct and painkiller haziness, I tried to extend my right hand, which was immobilized. Then I tried the left one. It took a few tries to convince the elbow to bend, but I think I managed not to wince too much.

Her hand seemed strong, a bit calloused, and she shook the hand just right—gently enough to respect the sore wrist, firmly enough that it didn't feel like she was condescending to the broken chick. Her nails were short and polished red.

"We've already gotten it as far as the porch. Might as well get rid of the coat." She shed her bulky peacoat. Underneath it, she wore a red knit dress, gray tights—and hiking boots.

My half-glazed eyes focused on the hiking boots. Lucia caught it and laughed. "Not exactly a fashion statement, but I'm not going to move a sofa in heels. Or walk to work in them, for that matter."

"Do you..." I hesitated for a second, my foggy brain derailed by the idea of her taking off that dress in my bedroom. I was in no shape to do anything about it, but I could probably manage to enjoy the view. "Want something to change into?"

She shrugged and chuckled. "The tights are old and the dress is washable."

And that was when I fell a bit in lust with Lucia.

No, I really fell for the way she muscled the sofa up the stairs, moving her end at least as easily as the much larger Nate did his. The way she treated the pretty dress as casually as I'd treat jeans and a sweatshirt simply sealed the deal. I have a weakness for femmes, but show me someone who can rock that look while wearing hiking boots and moving heavy objects and I'm doomed.

I had high hopes when Nate convinced her to stay for dinner. Normally I can hold my own in the flirtation game, even against Nate, who's an equal-opportunity lech (boys, girls and the occasional unwary artichoke), and hot enough that even I notice. But when you're attempting to impress a lovely lady, it helps if you don't nod off drooling over dinner.

Which I did, more than once. And Nate's dinners are worth staying awake for; I swear half the reason I'm friends with the man is that he cooks so well.

Meanwhile, Nate was on a roll, being Mr. Charm, saying and doing all the things I should have been doing to seduce Lucia. No great surprise, then, that they tucked me into bed and then went off to bed themselves.

The interesting noises wafting up from Nate's part of the house infiltrated my drugged dreams. By morning, I couldn't tell you what I'd dreamed, except that it had involved Lucia and left me very, very wet.

None of that surprised me.

Given Nate's history of flings and open friends-with-benefits arrangements, it did surprise me when Lucia starting turning up weekend after weekend at our place. Once in a while he had a hot-sex date with someone else during the week, usually one of his male fuck-buddies, but that got rarer and rarer as late winter moved into spring.

It was nice in a way, because at least once a weekend, we'd all have dinner together or do something as a group, but it was definitely frustrating. The more I got to know Lucia the more I liked that combination of girly and strong, dressed up and down to earth. We both came from rural backgrounds—my folks had an apple orchard in New York, hers grew organic vegetables in

California. Like me, she missed the country and was glad to be away from it in equal measure.

And let's face it, the shallower part of me loved that I never knew whether she'd turn up in jeans and boots, ready to help with the endless projects around the duplex, or in some fabulous dress ready to party—or if she'd show up all girlified and end up taking a few minutes to fix some minor thing that had just broken.

A hot, dressed-to-impress femme with a screwdriver: be still my beating clit.

If Nate was in his typical tomcat mode, I'd feel no qualms about hitting on one of his playmates. We'd casually dated the same woman in the past, and it had worked fine until she got tired of us being closer to each other than either of us was to her. But if he'd decided he was semi-quasi-serious about someone at last, I wasn't going risk messing things up, either by distracting Lucia or by making it uncomfortable for her to come around.

Damn. I hate being honorable sometimes.

As Nate's best buddy, I was delighted for him. As someone with a wicked crush, not so much. I figured, though, the crush would abate in time. They always did.

And it might have, too, if in the spring, when my arm was finally healed, Lucia hadn't offered to help us turn our shabby backyard into a garden. I'd thought about it since we'd moved in—helping in the garden had always been my favorite chore as a kid—but the idea of starting from scratch in a yard made of rubble and fill daunted me.

Nothing, apparently, daunted Lucia. Raised beds, she said, were the answer. (As soon as she said it, I kicked myself, realizing I should have thought of it.) Nate ordered a delivery of topsoil. Lucia and I agreed to go to Home Depot and buy some lumber.

It was a weeknight and we headed out to the suburbs after work. She wore a dress and heels and talked lumber with the Home Depot clerk in a way that would have impressed my uncle, who ran the lumberyard back in Seneca Falls. It went straight to my pussy.

I offered to work with her on the raised beds. "Nate's only a tool-user in the kitchen," I joked, which was true, but had very little to do with my motivation. A raised bed was the only bed I was likely to share with Lucia, so I'd take what I could get.

We didn't talk much as we worked, just about how best to anchor the wooden frames in place and level them on distinctly unlevel ground. She was busy, focused.

I was staring at her hands and imagining them on my body, just as skillful as they were with tools. All the time I was driving rebar into the hard soil and digging and hammering, my mind was definitely elsewhere. Even with Nate and me doing the basic cleanup during the week, it took a full weekend to finish those beds and load them up with topsoil. I don't think I had a clean thought the entire time.

Except when Nate came out to see if we needed food and gave Lucia a hug and a kiss and a playful grope. Then I guiltily tried not to think how much I wished I was the one molesting her.

The next weekend it was time to plant, and it was unreasonably, unseasonably warm.

On planting morning, Ben pulled up in his pickup truck and honked just as I'd meandered downstairs to collect Lucia and Nate for garden duty. (Lucia was wearing jeans and a T-shirt, but the T-shirt was bright pink and fitted, if obviously old—as close to girly as you can get doing serious gardening. It matched her garden clogs.) Nate grinned; gave Lucia a hard, quick kiss; grabbed an overnight bag and raced for the door.

As an afterthought, he waved at me. Then he stopped in his

tracks. "Sorry, Allie. I'm a dope—I forgot to tell you I had a last-minute chance to go out to P-town with Ben. I'll be back Sunday night. Have fun getting dirty without me, ladies." He leered as he said it, but Nate leered a lot. Even at artichokes.

We said good-bye and filed out to the garden, where our seedlings awaited us. I'd seethed quietly at first, but finally I let loose. "He's my best friend," I said, "but he can be such an asshole sometimes. He knew we have all these seedlings to get in."

Lucia shrugged. "I told him to go. He'll be useful in the garden when it starts producing food. Meanwhile, he's kind of clueless and underfoot and you know what you're doing. Besides, he's way past due for a boy-date."

I gaped like a fish and Lucia laughed at my expression. "Come on, you've known Nate for a million years. Did you honestly think he'd gone monogamous?"

"I wasn't sure, but you've been keeping him pretty busy."

"And he's been keeping me pretty busy, too. He's a lot of fun. But he's not the only interesting resident of this house, you know."

She said it lightly, but the sultry look in her dark eyes wasn't the one that went with telling a friend, "It's cool hanging out with you."

Sometimes I need a clue-by-four, but that was a clue-by-sixteen.

Lucia liked me.

And if Nate was off banging Ben this weekend with Lucia's blessing, then I could stop feeling guilty for my crush and finally kiss the woman.

Which I did.

As soon as I touched her, even before our lips met, all my pent-up desire bubbled to the surface. My heart raced, my stomach lurched, my nipples jumped.

And when her sweet lips parted for me, it took all my strength of will not to wrestle her down into the garden. That was moving a bit too fast, and besides we'd left some seedlings outside overnight to harden off and I'd hate to roll onto them. Instead I groaned into her mouth and wrapped my arms around her. She fit against me just perfectly, breast to breast, hip to hip, lip to lip, like we'd been created to facilitate making out.

When she pulled away, I felt like crying. But it was only so she could set down the flat of peppers we'd been crunching between us. They didn't look too damaged, but replacing them would be a small price to pay.

We have a nice high fence, but until Lucia starting hanging around, the yard wasn't exactly a location to inspire romantic, erotic thoughts, more like groans about whose turn it was to mow. I'd never thought of making love out here and I doubted Nate, horndog though he was, had either. But Lucia and I had worked hard to make it nice and would be working more to finish the job. Why not enjoy it?

I asked, "Do you want to go inside or stay out here?"

In response, she peeled off her T-shirt, exposing a blue bra that was more like ribbons, scraps of lace and the power of suggestion. If I'd thought for a moment she hadn't planned this, probably with Nate's eager collusion, that bra gave the preplanning away. I don't care how girly you are; that's a bra you put on hoping someone will see it. No, expecting someone will see it.

Looking was a treat but touching would be better and I wanted to get to it.

First things first, though. I wiggled out of my shorts and T-shirt and tossed them in the general direction of the steps. (I missed. I didn't care.) The shirt was one of those with a built-in bra and I managed to get the panties off along with the shorts, so that left me naked beneath the morning sky for the first time in…well, ever. (I still had sneakers on. Impulsive al fresco sex was good. Cutting your foot open was bad, and I knew how much broken glass and other junk we'd found in the yard.) The warm spring air felt like a torrid caress now, thanks to Lucia's appreciative gaze. I think of myself as more cute than beautiful, but I keep in good shape and she seemed to like what she saw.

Liked it well enough to reach out and touch.

Lucia's hands were small and elegantly shaped, a little dirty from handling the flats of seedlings. They traveled over my skin and left heaven and small muddy streaks in their wake. When they reached my nipples I thought I would scream from the sweet, sharp pleasure. I didn't scream, but only because I kissed her again and kept my mouth busy.

Kissed her and touched her soft skin and the hard muscles underneath. Caressed her breasts through the delicate little bra, then managed by some miracle to get the bra off without looking as clumsy as I suddenly felt. Her nipples were big and promi-nent, mocha against her golden skin, and I licked and suckled at those delights until she was writhing and mewling. She wriggled out her jeans and a ridiculously tiny pair of lacy blue panties with a lot of eager help from me. I finally learned a justification for those ugly rubber garden clogs—it was easy to kick them off, take off the jeans, and then slip the foot-protection back on. (Since they were now the only thing on an otherwise nude Lucia, they looked a lot less ugly.) Naked, she straddled my thigh and slipped her leg between mine.

We ground together until I was sure everything in the universe danced in rhythm to the pulsing of my cunt.

But when she got her oh-so-clever hands into the act, I forced myself to break away.

It was hard to make myself do it. I knew how good Lucia was with her hands, and I'd spent a lot of time imagining how that might translate to the sexual arena. But I needed to. She'd met me when I was damaged goods, unable to fend for myself. I'd done my best to change that impression as quickly as I could and from what she'd said about my gardening skills, it had worked. Still, she had ended up doing a lot of what was usually my share of house chores until I was fully healed, not to mention picking up a lot of slack for my adorable but absentminded housemate.

Not this time. "Oh, no you don't," I said. "You always end up doing all the work around here. This time you get to relax and enjoy."

"For a while, at least."

"For a while," I conceded. Hey, if her OCD tendencies extended to sex, I'd hate to deprive her of her fun—and hate to miss out on the fun she could provide—but I wanted to see her limp and sated first.

Nate's big contribution to the backyard redesign was a cedar bench so we could sit outside and enjoy the garden once it was finished. I steered her toward it. When the back of her legs bumped the seat, she sat down—she didn't flop like I would, but sank down gracefully. I knelt before her. The mulch we'd spread around it at Lucia's instruction wasn't the most comfortable surface for kneeling. Normally I make sure there's a pillow handy before making this sort of sexy dramatic gesture, and I thought very briefly of bringing the party inside.

But warm earth and the green smells of spring scented the air, and the hot smell of sex rising from Lucia's body blended too perfectly. I kissed her again, putting all my long-suppressed desire into it. She moaned into my mouth. I could scarcely hear it, but I swear I could taste it.

I kissed my way down her body, paying special attention to her nipples again: first one then the other. God, they were more perfect than I'd imagined in my fantasies, plumper and darker and more sensitive. I could have spent hours sucking and teasing and nibbling and exploring, and if I was lucky enough for a second chance with her, I would. But the heady, rich scent of an aroused pussy was just too tempting to resist.

I sank down, getting better acquainted with the mulch than I'd ever meant to be, and got my face between Lucia's open legs.

Inhaled her warm, feminine, musky smell until I swore I was drunk on it.

Took a good look and enjoyed what I saw. She was clean shaven, her pussy lips as dark and delicious as her nipples and slick with juice. Her clit was swollen, a tempting little morsel all but quivering in anticipation of my tongue.

I thought about teasing her a little, a small revenge for all the months I had waited and dreamed and lusted, thinking she wasn't interested.

Then she breathed, "Please," and that game paled before the fun of making a beautiful woman scream.

I put one arm around her, pulled her forward (with her eager, squirming help) to reach my mouth more easily.

I could get all flowery and poetic and talk about oysters and musk or something like that, but what Lucia tasted like was an aroused woman on a warm spring day, rich and tangy and a little salty, delicious.

Her hands tangled in my hair. She rolled her hips, moving her pussy against my eager tongue. I spent some time indulging myself, exploring and enjoying getting to taste Lucia at last: savoring her scent and flavor, the little shudders when I hit just the perfect spot, the wonderfully erotic noises that I'd heard from Nate's place—and had masturbated to—so many times.

But as the shudders became contractions and the noises grew more frantic, I had to finish the job, had to make Lucia scream and sob with pleasure.

I slipped one finger inside her as I licked, then two. She was sleek and slippery and gripped my questing fingers, the muscles of her pussy as strong as her wiry arms. I caught her rhythm, pushed it.

"Please," she cried, and "Almost too much," and "Yes!"

Then she lost words and simply screamed and wailed as she bucked against my mouth and clamped down on my fingers.

I didn't stop until she grabbed my hair and moved me away.

"Good thing the neighbors are used to crazy noises from this house," I said, smiling what I knew had to be a terribly smug grin. "Otherwise they might call the cops."

"Confession time." Lucia's voice was still shaky, but her arms were strong around me. "Nate brought me around that first time planning to set me up with you. But you were in such rough shape I couldn't tell if we'd suit or not—I liked your looks, but you weren't exactly coherent. And Nate..."

"Did what Nate, from all reports, does best," I finished. "And by the time I wasn't the armless wonder, it seemed to be getting serious, so I didn't even try."

"It's heading toward serious. But neither of us is cut out for monogamy. It's something we've talked about a lot. I'm not sure how you two feel about dating the same person..."

"Wouldn't be the first time." But it would, I resolved, be the last—because Lucia was a keeper and one of us, if not both, should keep her. "Nate and I are family. Why not keep it in the family?"

"Good. Because I really like you both. Nate and I wanted to make sure we were solid before we went out to play again, or I'd have made a move before now. And it'll be good to get a break from him once in a while. He's a lot of fun, but he's kind of needy and greedy at times."

I dropped my voice to what I hoped was a sultry pitch. "Actually I'm feeling needy and greedy right now, and I could use some help from your clever hands."

She kissed me quick and hard, then said, "That kind of help I'm always happy to provide!"

NEVER
TOO OLD

DeJay

Y ou did what?"

"I just went online and got the address of Wild Hearts for you. It's on Commercial Street, right across from the Crown and Anchor, so I can wait there and have a drink while you pick up our purchases."

I looked at my wife, my partner of thirty-plus years, and couldn't believe what she had just said. "Why would you do that?"

She smiled at me—the little-girl grin, the one where her eyes twinkle and her dimples pop. "It'll be fun."

"Fun?" I felt like I didn't even know her.

She walked over and wrapped her arms around my neck. "It will be, I promise." With that she kissed me.

"I'm not so sure about this."

"Don't be a baby."

"Why do *I* have to go? *You're* the one who wants this stuff."

"Because they have to measure you, silly."

The glint in her eye had me wary. "Measure me?" I thought about that for a moment. "There?"

"No, you idiot, your hips and thighs." She turned and poured a cup of coffee; then, holding out the pot to me as if everything were perfectly normal, she asked, "Want some more?"

"No. Yes. Fuck." I looked at her closely for some hint, some idea as to what I had been doing wrong. "I thought we were okay in that department?"

She poured the coffee and looked up. "You know we are."

"I mean, we have sex at least twice a week, sometimes three, right?"

"It's not about that."

"I only fell asleep last week because I was exhausted, I swear."

"Honey, it's not about you falling asleep."

I started to sweat, trickles of moisture forming on my upper lip and around my hairline. "I thought, you know, that you enjoyed our sex life." Had she been faking it all this time?

Abby walked closer and cupped my jaw. "Honey, I do. We have a great sex life. This is just a little experiment, something to spice it up, that's all."

"Now? At our age?"

"We're not dead, you know, and I've been thinking about it for a while."

My insides were churning full blast now. "A while?"

"Remember a couple months ago when we had that problem with dryness?"

I thought back, then nodded. "You called the doctor, right?"

"Yes, but I also talked to Mary."

I groaned out loud.

"Stop it. We're all adults, and she and I are the same age, so it was perfectly natural to ask her."

I put my head in my hands, knowing I wouldn't like the rest of this conversation. "And?"

"And she had the same problem. Vic got her some lubricants."

I sat up straighter, immediately feeling better. "We did, too."

"Exactly, but did you know there are many kinds of lubricants? Some even flavored, for...you know. So we discussed that and other stuff."

"Fuck." I looked at her pleadingly.

"Stop it."

"Please tell me you did not discuss our sex life, I'm begging you."

"Grow up."

I put my head in my arms on the ceramic countertop where I was sitting. The day had started so nicely. I woke early, did the treadmill for an hour. I had an idea for a story I was excited about. With my laptop set up, I was working at the kitchen counter while the coffee perked and the dogs were outside napping. I even asked Abby to give me quiet time to write, and she had agreed, as usual, but not ten minutes she later came into the kitchen and made her announcement. And now this.

I took a deep breath. "And?"

"Well, when Mary and I talked, she told me that she and Vicky, they have one."

"Oh, fuck, you did not just tell me that." I rubbed my eyes desperately trying to erase that image of my best friend, with a strap-on, from my brain. "Why do you insist on telling me shit like this, why?"

"What is the big deal? It's perfectly normal."

I took a deep breath and twisted my neck from side to side, still trying to purge the image she had burned into my retinas.

"Normal, absolutely, but I do not ever want to think of my two best friends like that. Is that okay with you?"

"Why?"

"Because they're my friends, damn it."

"Don't be such a child." She rubbed my hand and grinned. "You can't get the image out of your mind, can you?"

I groaned out loud. She was right. "No, and I'm blaming you."

She started laughing, then stopped abruptly. She must have realized I was not finding this at all funny. "Okay, so it's a little embarrassing, but they're our friends."

"Tell me now, before I ever see Vicky again, did you tell Mary you want to do this?"

"*No*, of course not."

"You swear?"

"I swear." She crossed her heart. I *almost* believed her.

"I do not want another incident like when Mary told me about Vic wearing a damn nightgown."

Abby knew I still had trouble looking my best friend in the eye ever since her wife had revealed that little tidbit. Vic, a butch's butch if ever there was one, wore a pink-flowered, flannel nightgown. "Fuck, now I'm picturing her in the damn nightgown with a friggin strap-on underneath."

"Don't be silly."

"I'm not."

"So anyway, I've been thinking about it and decided our trip to P-town provides the perfect time for us to get equipped."

"Equipped?"

"Supplies."

I ran my hands through my hair. The world had gone mad, nothing was making any sense. "You're going with me. Why do I have to go in there alone?"

"Remember the Sears incident?"

I cringed. Years ago we had been shopping in Sears for Christmas presents. Abby found a robe she thought her mom would like and asked me to try it on to see if the length was okay since her mom and I had similar builds. There I was, dressed in my jeans, motorcycle boots, and a leather jacket. It was a simple, stupid cotton garment with lace around the collar. Once I had it on, Abby started laughing and wouldn't stop. She swore she had images of what our future held. The angrier I got, the more she laughed; the more she laughed, the more she alerted our fellow shoppers, who then started staring and laughing as well. I tore the damn thing off and never helped her again for fear of that kind of humiliation.

"I ordered everything from the catalogue. All you have to do is let them make sure the harness is the right size, and then you can pay for it all and leave. Simple."

Abby stood there angelically smiling. I was sure I was missing something. "You already ordered what you want, right?"

"Yup."

"All I have to do is check on the size of the harness, right?"

"Absolutely."

"Ten minutes tops?"

"Less."

"What if someone I know is in the store?"

"Say hi."

I shook my head. "You know what I mean. How am I going to explain why I'm there?"

"What do you think *they* would be doing there?"

I covered my ears. "Fuck, I do not want to think about that."

"Stop being ridiculous. I think it's wonderful people our age are willing to experiment."

"Why exactly are we experimenting again?"

"Because I don't want you bored."

"Please tell me what's really going on here?"

Abby leaned in close and kissed me. "I don't want you trading me in for three twenties."

Each time she hit another milestone in age, she decided I would trade her in for X number of younger women. At thirty, it was two fifteen-year-olds. I pointed out that would be jailbait. At forty, it was two twenty-year-olds; I asked what the hell I would do with them. At fifty, she announced two twenty-five year-olds, because I was older and needed to slow down. Now at sixty, *this*.

"I love you, I can barely keep up with you. Have you talked to a twenty-year-old of late? I don't even understand their language."

"It's not you having a conversation with them I'm worried about."

"Abbs, I've never given you reason to worry, have I?"

She kissed me again. "And I intend to make sure you want to come home to me and only me."

"Now who's being childish?"

"Please, it's important to me."

I sighed, knowing I had lost this battle many, many minutes ago. "Quick in and out, right?"

"I promise."

"Let's get going, you have a one o'clock appointment with Cheryl."

"Cheryl?" I was towel-drying my hair after my shower.

"The store, Wild Hearts."

I glanced in the mirror, catching her eyes. "I need an appointment to shop?"

"Well, it's their personalized service. I thought you would like that."

"Oh. Okay." I folded the towel and put it on the tub, then grabbed my T-shirt and pulled it on.

"Make sure you wear boxers today."

"Huh?"

"Just do it."

"Why?"

Abby was applying mascara; she looked in the mirror at me. "So I don't have to worry about you."

I walked toward her, my jeans in one hand, naked from the waist down. "I thought you liked it when I went commando."

"Not today."

She had been in a funny mood ever since we arrived in P-town. This morning after breakfast, instead of us sightseeing, she had wanted to come back here and make love. I was up for that but she still seemed edgy, even afterward.

"Okay, boxers it is."

Abby leaned over, grabbed a pair out of the duffle bag and handed them to me.

"You're lucky I packed some."

"No. You are, or you'd be wearing a pair of my panties."

"Like hell."

She just giggled and returned to putting on her makeup.

Once I was dressed, she turned to me. "You look nice."

I looked down and frowned. I was only wearing jeans and that T-shirt. "Thanks?"

"I just wanted to tell you."

I put my arms around her and kissed her. "I love you, with all my heart. Thank you."

"Come on, I want to get a seat at the bar."

I glanced at the alarm clock on the nightstand. "It's only

twelve thirty."

"I know, but you know I like sitting where I can see the TV. I want to get there before it fills up."

Abby was a sports nut. She always wanted to be in front of the big-screen TV so she could watch the latest action, no matter what the sport. "I'm ready."

As I held the door for Abbs outside the restaurant, she practically squealed. "Oh, look! Two seats right up front. Excellent."

We walked directly to the bar and ordered drinks. Abby asked for a draft, while I got a Coke. I was doing a reading at Gabriel's at the Ashbrooke Inn later that evening and didn't want to screw it up by being tipsy or, worse, drunk. I glanced at the menu. "Want to get something? I'm kinda hungry."

"Eat when you get back. You can't be late."

"Jesus, why not? Won't our money be just as good if I'm late, say twenty minutes or so?"

"You can wait and be back here in the same twenty minutes."

"I thought you said quick in and out."

"I'm giving you time to walk across the street and back again...you *are* getting older."

I love Abby with all my heart, but something had the hairs on my neck on end. "You ordered everything, right?"

"Yup."

"I don't have to ask for anything special, right?"

"Absolutely. Just let them determine the right size harness and you're out of there."

I couldn't find any hidden meaning or problem in her words, so I nodded. "Okay. Keep the chair warm for me."

She leaned over and kissed my cheek. "You're my *she*ro."

"Yeah, yeah." I took a deep breath and headed to Wild Hearts.

Outside the store, I took another deep breath and sent up a prayer that no one I knew would be inside. I pushed through the entrance and gasped. Dildos lined the walls, dildos in all shapes, sizes and colors. On the top shelf, a sign announced, VIBRATORS OPTIONAL. Another sign declared JUST RIGHT FOR THE G-SPOT. Some were remote control, some even glowed in the dark. I didn't know where to look, and everywhere I turned my head, I was barraged with other sex toys—instruments of lust in all shapes, sizes and, lord help me, for all purposes.

"May I help you?"

I turned to find a child/woman standing before me. "What are you, ten?"

She grinned. "I'm actually twenty-two. Is there something I can help you with?"

"Appointment...I mean, I have an appointment."

"Do you know with whom?" She said the words slowly as if I wouldn't comprehend.

"Yes." I nodded my head.

She smiled at me knowingly. "Do you *know* her name?"

I nodded again. I did know. "Cheryl. It's Cheryl."

"Good. I'll get her for you. Don't go anywhere."

I shoved my hands in my pockets and tried not to stare at things. I just knew someone I knew was going to find me in here.

"Hello, I'm Cheryl, can I help you?"

Another child stood before me. This one appeared even younger. "Are you Cheryl?"

"I thought we had established that. Yes, I am." She held out her hand.

"I have an appointment."

"And you are?"

I took a ragged breath. "Your one o'clock appointment."

"It's your first time isn't it?" She took my arm and pulled me toward a counter in the front of the store. Once there she opened an appointment book and looked down. "You're Ms. Michaels then?"

"Dani. Dani Michaels."

"See, that wasn't so hard."

I tried to relax, but it was useless. "My wife, she told me you have everything ready, just need to be sure of the size of the belt, right?"

"Belt?"

I felt my cheeks turning red, starting to burn. "Harness, I meant harness."

Cheryl grinned. "Yes. Let's go into the dressing room. That way we can have some privacy."

"Privacy?"

She was walking in front of me toward the back of the store. "Well, I can't very well measure you over your jeans." We had just passed an entire display case of edible clothing—bras, panties, nipple covers. I averted my eyes quickly, hoping to avoid discovering anything else. No such luck. Before me stood a rack of ladies' underthings: corsets, lace bras, nippleless bras, satin and lace camisoles and garter sets and on and on it went.

"Right in here. Please take you pants off."

It was futile. I had turned beet red, I just knew it. This girl had to be a teenager, and she was telling me to take my pants off. I had to be breaking some law.

"Uh, I could do the measurements and just call them out to you."

"Don't be shy, I do this all the time." With that she sat in the chair staring at me.

I knew my fate had been cast. I unbuckled my belt and opened the button, then slid the zipper downward and stepped out of my jeans. In the mirror I caught a glance at myself and wanted the floor to open up. I was wearing my Sponge-Bob boxers. I was going to kill Abby when I saw her.

"Yes, I can see why your wife was concerned. You do have big thighs."

"Does this mean you can't fit me?" I surged with hope.

"Not at all. I just need to get a different size, then I'll bring your purchases in and go over them with you. I'll be just a moment."

Cheryl stepped out of the room, so I grabbed my jeans and slipped them on. I'd be damned if we were going to discuss anything with me undressed.

I was just buckling my belt when she stepped back in.

Cheryl looked at me. "Is something wrong?"

"No."

"Why did you get dressed?"

"You said you knew the size I needed."

Cheryl held up the item in question. "I need to see it on you, show you how to use it, load it. Make sure it's tight enough to hold, but loose enough for comfort."

"Oh." I undid my belt; Sponge-Bob would make another appearance.

"I'd like to suggest a larger size in jeans from now on."

"What? Why?"

"You need to allow room for the harness and accessory."

"Huh?"

"Well, I assumed you'd be wearing it on dates and such, or on special occasions."

"I don't date. I'm married."

"I meant when you and your wife go out."

"In public, you mean?" The room was definitely getting hotter.

"If you went up a size in your jeans, no one would know but you and your lady."

"In *public*?"

She looked at me pityingly. "Lots of butches do."

Cheryl turned and started unpacking a shopping bag the size of a small minivan. What the fuck had Abby purchased?

"The three various attachments your wife picked out all work lovely with this belt. As I told her, leather is the way to go. Much sturdier and so many options." Cheryl glanced up and smiled.

"Uh-huh."

"Now this particular one is a favorite of mine."

Cheryl removed from the bag what looked like a penis with a long handle attached. *What would...how would... Holy crap, that is not a handle.*

"Your wife was very excited that we had it in stock." Cheryl held up the dual dildo. "This is our best seller. It's called the Nexus. As you can see, the two of you will simultaneously receive enjoyment from this model."

"Uh-huh."

"Here, let's get the harness on you first, then I can show you how to load it."

"What?"

"I want to be sure it fits properly. Then we can experiment with the various attachments."

The room was getting warmer and smaller all at once. "Fine."

As Cheryl painstakingly fit the harness over my boxers, she continued her lesson. "Your wife was such a joy to talk to. She had done her research and knew exactly what she was looking for. We spoke on the phone for over an hour. "

"I'll bet."

"Seriously, you'd be surprised how many women have no

idea, and then I have to show and explain all the options." Cheryl tugged on the now-secured harness. "I think that's got it for you. How does it feel?"

"I'm not sure how to answer that."

"It's got to be tight enough to sustain the thrusting motion, but not so tight as to cause chafing or sores."

"We can adjust it, right?"

"Oh, yes, this model is perfect for that."

I looked down, gave it a tug. "Okay, I guess."

Cheryl turned to the little table behind her and picked up the Nexus, the double dildo, the mutual satisfaction one. *Crap.*

"Now this one should be inserted this way into the harness first, then be sure to lubricate your end and slip it in as you're tightening the straps on the harness. Shall I demonstrate? I have some lube here."

"No! No...I'll...figure it out, thanks."

She shrugged. "Okay. Just let me show you how to secure the dildo into the harness then. Oh, I better use the other model." She pulled out a shiny pink wobbly one and inserted a battery pack in it. "This is the G-Pulse Dildo attachment. It's battery operated and sure to give you both a little extra sensation. Plus, it's perfect for the G-spot. Also, it's made of soft gel versus the silicone models. It won't last as long, but it's wonderfully soft and pliable, as you can see."

The damn thing was wiggling like a Jell-O mold. I was afraid it would melt.

"Always be sure to get the rim flush against the harness here, see?" She had loosened one strap and inserted the attachment. It now hung in front of me like a body extension.

"How many of these did Abby buy, exactly?"

Cheryl looked up and grinned. "Just one more...another popular one with the femmes. It's called the Bandito. She chose lavender, but she especially liked the contour and shape of that one."

"She did, huh?"

"As I said, your wife was a delight, very knowledgeable. It's a shame she couldn't make the trip with you."

"Yes. Yes, it is." All the pieces were finally coming together. Abby might be a tiger in bed, but she turns red at off-color jokes. On the other hand she knows her shortcomings; this place would be like a candy store to her. She would want to look at everything to learn how it works.

"Now, you're aware that the two silicone models can be put into the dishwasher for sterilization, right? For the soft-gel model we recommend you use prophylactics to ensure cleanliness."

"You mean rubbers?"

"Yes."

I just shook my head. I was going to kill Abby. Kill her dead.

After twenty minutes of me proving I could properly load and unload the various dildos, Cheryl finally let me take off the harness. "We're doing so well. Now have you ever used the Tongue Joy vibrator?"

"I'm almost afraid to ask."

Cheryl chuckled softly. "It's a vibrator for your tongue."

"Can I get electrocuted?"

"No, it uses batteries and is quite safe and small."

"I'll probably end up swallowing it."

Cheryl just smiled. "Here, let me show you how it works."

I stepped back. "I think I can figure that out. Is there anything else in there?"

"Yes, we still have the video your wife thought you should watch, and I have two models of vibrators she ordered. One for your finger, the Fun Fingazs Vibe, and one she inserts, the Pocket Rocket model."

"Inserts?"

"Yes. Some women like to keep stimulated while working or shopping."

I thought my head was going to explode. "Is it safe? You know, for a woman to stay stimulated like that?"

"It's wonderful. I have one in right now and love it. So does my wife when I get home, if you know what I mean."

That was it. I closed my eyes to the image of children having sex. I now knew I had definitely broken some kind of federal law. I was waiting for the store to be raided and me whisked away in handcuffs.

"So shall we head to the viewing room?"

"The what?"

"It's where you can watch the video in comfort. Afterward you can ask me questions and I'll answer them for you."

"I can't believe I'm going to ask this, but what kind of video is this?"

Cheryl gave me a patronizing smile. "An instructional one, though we do have others if you're interested in that kind of thing."

"No. No, that's fine. In fact I think I'll let my wife watch the video with me, and if she has any questions she can always call you later, right?"

"Of course. I'll take this up front. When you're ready, come to the counter and I'll ring you up."

After she left the dressing room, I banged my head on the wall three or four times. I could not believe Abby had set me up like this. She knew. She knew and still she sent me in here alone. I slipped back into my jeans and headed to the front of the store. The sooner I paid for this stuff, the quicker I could get out of there, hopefully without anyone discovering me there.

I stepped outside and took a deep breath. My insides were

shaking, and I was more determined to kill Abby then ever. I was now saddled with a small human-size shopping bag that had the name of the boutique emblazoned in red letters across it. I looked both ways, trying to figure out what to do, where to stash the bag. Then it hit me.

I trotted into the restaurant. Abby was engrossed in a football game and cheering along with the other women alongside her. I walked up behind her and placed the bag on the bar. "Here's your purchases, sweetie."

Abby turned, saw the name on the bag, and grabbed it off the countertop. "Are you crazy?"

I smiled evilly. "No, baby, I just wanted you to have the full experience." I sat down next to her and let her deal with the satchel.

Abby looked at me from the corner of her eye, trying to hide the bag between herself and the wall. "You're mad?"

"Nope."

"What took so long?"

"As if you don't know."

She turned to face me, her expression blank. "I don't."

"Don't lie, sweetheart, Cheryl gave you up."

Now it was Abby's turn to blush. "I'm really not sure what you mean."

"Let me explain it." Just then Jillian, the bartender, stepped up. "Another Coke please, and some wings for two."

"Be right back."

I turned back to Abby, lowered my voice. "As I was saying, not only did Cheryl have to measure me, but then she proceeded to strap me in and demonstrate how every fucking thing you bought is used."

Abby tried to smother her laughter.

"I'm not amused, Abbs."

"She really demonstrated it? Everything?"

"Oh, yeah." My temper finally kicked in. "I'm can honestly say I feel quite confident that I can pack any dildo into the harness without a hitch, that I know exactly how to wash and care for the models you purchased—three by the way, is that right? I also am quite positive that I know how and where the tongue and finger vibrators go and how to use them. We have lubricants in three flavors, all water based, and I know that the raspberry flavor is the most natural-tasting one. I am assured you will be safe stimulating yourself while out in public with your little Pocket Rocket...oh, and I need to buy bigger jeans. How's that for a synopsis?"

Too late, I realized my voice had risen in my fervor to make Abby understand my complete and total mortification. I hadn't paid attention to the fact that the volume on the TVs had been muted, that the eyes of the other patrons were trained on us, or that Jillian was standing there with our appetizers.

A thunderous round of applause broke out at the bar as I concluded my speech. Abby did what I had wanted to do earlier; she ran out of the bar as fast as she could, leaving me to carry the bag back to the hotel room.

"Oh. My. God."

I lifted my head and smiled up from between Abby's legs.

"That was the best sex ever."

I swiped my tongue one more time up through her folds, then climbed up next to her and kissed her on the lips. "Pretty good, huh?"

Abby grinned. "Better than good, perfect."

I rolled over onto my back and pulled her snugly up against me.

"Feeling pretty good about yourself, aren't you?"

"Absolutely. And it was all me, no damn gadgets."

Abby laughed out loud. "Yes it was, and it was wonderful."

"See, I told you we didn't need this stuff."

"I'm sorry I laughed."

I glanced at her. "Yeah, well, I guess if you didn't know what to expect, it was a little silly looking."

"It was as if it had a life of its own."

"I guess I didn't tighten it enough. But you didn't need to laugh."

"You looked so miserable."

"It's not that bad, just takes some getting used to, I guess."

Abby started caressing my chest. "Does that mean you're willing to try again?"

"Not if you're going to laugh."

"I promise not to, not now that I know how it looks." She kissed me. "Please?"

"I guess. It's not like I have to go shopping. We already have everything...might as well get our money's worth."

Abby sat up. "Come on, I'll help you this time. You can show me what you learned."

"Now?"

"Yes, now."

"But we just did it."

"And now we're going to do it again."

"Twice in one day?" I looked at her incredulously. "At our age?"

"Do you feel old right now?"

I jumped up and went across the room to where I had flung the harness. "So which model do you want tonight, my dear?"

"I'm feeling a little naughty. Let's try the Bandito, shall we?"

"You had to get the lavender one...you couldn't get the black one?"

"Are you going to complain or put it to use?"

"I can't wait to have your mother find one of these in the dishwasher."

LOST AND FOUND

Andrea Dale

An all-expenses-paid trip to Hawaii? Sign me up!

So what if I got slammed with a massive last-minute freelance accounting job from a well-paying but notoriously flaky client the day before we left? But hey—have laptop, will travel. I could make my deadline if I hunkered down in the hotel room.

Except for when I snuck out to take surfing lessons from some sloe-eyed, sultry native pro...

I went from that lovely fantasy on the plane to standing forlornly in the baggage claim area, watching the empty carousel go round and round.

The airline folks wrung their hands. *So sorry,* they said. *Really feel bad about this,* they insisted. *We'll do everything in our power to find the suitcase,* they promised, *but there's only one flight to this island per day,* they apologized, *so it may take time....*

"Oh, my god, Lara, I'm so sorry!" Jeanne's eyes were wide with compassion. She hated traveling—which was why she'd asked me to tag along while she gave a workshop at the annual Women's Proactive Retreat and Conference—and this was a personal nightmare of hers, ranking right up there with being thrown in a Thai prison for accidentally smuggling drugs.

"I'll be okay," I said, putting on my gamest smile. "I've got a change of underwear and a toothbrush in my carry-on, at least. That'll get me through."

I could handle this. I squared my shoulders. I've backpacked around Europe for six months, I've boated down the Grand Canyon for sixteen days with only what I could carry. I could make do until they found my luggage.

I'd pick up a few essentials at a discount store—they did have Target here, right? Or at least Walmart?—and get by.

Or so I thought.

No, the smaller islands didn't have discount stores (what was I thinking?). And we were bussed right out to the resort, where my only option was the gift shop—in which the cheapest T-shirt was more than I'd be willing to spend on a new dress.

Let's not talk about how much the dresses cost.

Not to mention the bathing suits. There was a gorgeous shimmery copper one, sturdy enough for laps in the pool but pretty enough to catch the eye, but it was far, far out of my budget.

The next morning I poked at my travel shirt, which I'd hand-washed the night before. Still damp.

About the only positive thing I could grasp on to right now was the fact that the hotel rooms had nice gushy complimentary robes. I ordered the cheapest thing I could get by on from room service, wincing at the cost, but I couldn't go wandering down to the dining room in the robe, you know? Hopefully Jeanne would swing by before lunch and have time to grab something for me.

The accounting books, as usual, had not only been late, but

were a mess. I scowled. I couldn't even escape from them for a swim or a walk to ogle sloe-eyed, sultry natives....

There was a knock at the door. Couldn't housekeeping see the bloody DO NOT DISTURB sign? As tempting as it was, I was too polite to shout, "Go away!" so I opened the door.

Well, hello. Apparently my despair had been a call, because a sloe-eyed, sultry native had come to me.

She wore adorable little black rectangle glasses and a cool white wraparound top that showed just a hint of cleavage, as well as a Women's Conference badge.

My heart leapt. "They've found my luggage?" I leaned out to peer behind her.

"No, I'm sorry," she said. "I'm Evie, with the conference. Your partner told me about your missing suitcase."

"Jeanne's not my partner," I said, because suddenly that was a much more important fact to clarify than the whereabouts of any silly suitcase. "We're just good friends."

"Oh!" said the delectable Evie. "Oh. I'm sorry."

I laughed. "Really, not a problem. What can I do for you?"

I tried not to think too hard about what I really wanted to do for her. Or to her. Damn, but I didn't normally fall in lust so...instantaneously.

But she had the cutest dimple, and I just wanted to lick it, for starters.

"I wanted to help you out," she said. "If you'll give me your sizes, I'll ask around and see if any of the other attendees have clothes you could borrow. Or maybe take up a collection so you could buy a few things." She leaned in conspiratorially; I smelled a fruity sort of perfume or maybe sunscreen. "The prices in the gift shop are just *insane*."

Thank god it wasn't just me.

I backed up to let her in. "I'd feel really weird if people paid for my clothes," I said. "I'm not even attending the conference."

She collapsed onto the bed, her skirt riding up to show a yummy expanse of tanned, toned leg. "I see your point," she said, "but I think it would actually make them feel good. Helping a sista, don't'cha know."

I laughed. "True. But I really don't need a new wardrobe; I just need a few things to get me by until my luggage arrives."

"I like you," Evie said, flashing that damn dimple again. "You have a highly developed sense of optimism."

"If I didn't laugh, I'd have to cry," I said. "Why doesn't this island have a Kmart?"

"Hm," Evie said. "There *is* a lone dollar-store-type place two towns over. It's pretty cheesy, but it might do the trick."

She'd be able to steal a couple of hours after lunch, and so I worked like a fiend to get as much number-crunching done as I could before then.

That was hard, because my mind kept wandering back to Evie and that dimple and the way she'd said, "I like you," and even though I had no idea if she liked girls, I was imagining her straddling me, saying, "I like you," as she dipped down for a kiss, or pinned beneath me, saying, "I like you," as I feasted on her pert nipples. (Score one for the air-conditioning in my hotel room, which had left me pretty certain she hadn't been wearing a bra.)

That lack of bra continued to work to my advantage, because journeying two towns away involved driving over some bumpy dirt roads. I watched out of the corner of my eye while keeping up my end of the conversation.

I was thrilled when, in answer to my question, "What do you do for fun?" she said she surfed.

"That's something I've always wanted to try," I said. "I've waterskiied...is it very different?"

"There's more balance needed, but if you have the basic

skills, it's not that hard," she said. She flashed that dimple again. "If you're free Sunday afternoon and the conditions are good, I'd be happy to show you the ropes."

Oh, I'd be free, all right. I'd stay up all Saturday night working if I had to.

Then we got to the dollar store, and all bets were off again. They didn't have any bathing suits.

I came away with a couple of Hawaiian-print sarong-type skirts and some basic T-shirts in matching colors, which would get me through the rest of my stay. The only beachwear they had were a couple of eensy bikinis, and I'd have had to sew at least three of the bra cups together to cover one of my generous womanly gifts.

I grabbed an extra T-shirt, a hot-pink touristy thing that proclaimed ALOHA! in exuberant swirly aqua print. Maybe I could get away with it and a pair of panties for a midnight dip in the ocean when nobody else was around.

On the way back, we stopped at what looked like a ramshackle shack teetering precariously on a cliff, but in fact was a restaurant serving the best fish tacos on the planet. I swear I wanted to be alone with mine.

But I *was* alone with it—and with Evie—and that was even better.

As she gazed out over the view that I admitted was spectacular, though not as spectacular as she was, I wondered again whether she liked girls.

It was now or never. I refused to run from a challenge. "Thank you," I said, and then I leaned over and brushed a kiss across her cheek, inhaling that sweet sunscreen scent.

If she didn't get it, so be it.

She got it. As I drew away, she turned her head. Our lips were inches apart.

"Oh," she said, curving her mouth in a naughty, dimpled grin. "Do that like you mean it."

Could anyone refuse an invitation like that? I brushed my fingers along her jaw, urging her closer, watching her until her eyes fluttered shut and our lips met. Then I couldn't keep my eyes open, either.

She tasted like salsa, hot and spicy. Our tongues met, flirted, succumbed to the age-old dance.

On the table, our fingers twined. A slow, warm glow started in my belly, spreading lower as if I were bathed in sunlight from the inside. My nipples tightened and my groin followed suit, pressure building.

Just from that kiss.

Finally, reluctantly, she pulled away. "Wow," she said. "I hope that was as amazing for you as it was for me."

All I could do was nod.

"I wish I could sit here and kiss you for hours," she went on, "but I'm afraid I've got to get back...." Her hand squeezed mine. "Can I see you tonight?"

Again, nodding was my only available option. She'd left me speechless with delight.

I realized, as I tried to focus on work and failed miserably, that I was nervous. Why, I wasn't entirely sure. She was cute, she was interested in me; what was the problem?

The problem was that I really *liked* her. I'd never been into flings per se, but there had been times when the planets aligned and I'd had a juicy time with a like-minded girl, no strings attached.

Evie lived in Hawaii (on Oahu, granted) and I was from Chicago. What kind of future could we have?

And why was I thinking about the future anyway?

* * *

After the dry air-conditioning in the hotel, the sultry night air was a relief, soft and sweet smelling against my skin. I was to meet Evie in one of the cabanas, far down the beach. The closer cabanas were filled with women who'd spilled out after the conference activities officially ended at ten; I found Evie in a more secluded one, with its own little cove.

She'd laid out leftover hors d'oeuvres from the conference, along with a bottle of wine and a multitude of candles.

I was hungry—to keep the cost down I'd been getting most of my meals out of the vending machines—but at the same time, I didn't want to eat too much. I nibbled juicy chunks of pineapple and mango, tasted spicy shrimp skewers and let sweet wine and conversation flow.

Finally, though, before I could talk myself out of it, I leaned in and kissed her again.

Her skin was salty and sun warmed even now, this late, and I was shaking right down to my dollar-store panties, a heady combination of nerves and lust.

The nerves mostly faded as the kiss progressed, thanks to her enthusiasm. It's hard to have self-doubts when someone's kissing you with so much fervor that you nearly fall off your chair.

When we broke apart, we were both breathless.

"I have something for you," she said.

"I bet you do," I murmured.

She laughed. "That's not what I mean—not right now, anyway. Here."

She held up a resort-logoed bag. Inside, I found the shimmery copper bathing suit from the hotel gift shop.

"Some of the women heard about your luggage and had already started pooling their money," she said before I could protest. "Anyway, it's for tomorrow. For when I give you your surfing lesson." In the candlelight, I saw the wicked glint in her eye. "Tonight, though, you won't be needing it. Up for a swim?"

If I'd been thinking more clearly, I would've understood that she was suggesting skinny-dipping—which I had no problem with any time—but when she pulled her top over her head, my tongue stuck to the roof of my mouth.

Her tanned skin gleamed in the candle flames, and from the lack of lines, I knew she didn't wear a suit very often even in the daylight.

Stop staring and strip. Stop ogling her teardrop breasts and thinking about how you want to take those fat nipples into your mouth.

I compromised and multitasked: I stripped while fantasizing and catching glances as often as I could.

The water was so calm, so utterly smooth and pristine that I felt a pang of reluctance at disturbing it. But Evie grabbed my hand and urged, "Come on," and then we were running out together, laughing as the sand shifted beneath our feet and the drag of the water slowed us down.

We dove and swam and bobbed in the amazingly warm, buoyant water, and when we paused to catch our breaths, I licked her dimple and kissed her again.

She was saltier and wetter, but her tongue was warm as we got more serious. I was through playing, done with questioning myself—now I wanted her, and I wanted her now.

I pressed against her. She was taller than me, but the ocean's effect on my breasts meant they were pretty much in line with hers. I moaned into her mouth when I felt my nipples press against her and hers against me.

Bliss.

Beneath the soft water, she slid her hands over my hips, into my waist and up between us, gently urging me back so she could cup my breasts. She rolled my nipples between her fingers, gently at first and then harder as I hissed "Yes. *Yes,*" and the sweet electric shocks of pleasure rippled through me.

I sank my teeth into her lower lip, not hard, just tugging and sucking. It wasn't enough, so I backed toward shallower waters, just enough so her torso was exposed and I could feast on her the way she had touched me. Her mews of delight made my head swim. I could've nipped and licked forever, just to hear her gasp and beg for more.

More was what we both wanted, almost to the point of frenzy. I molded my hands to her pert ass, slid lower. The water was warm, but her core was molten like the volcanoes that had formed this island. I wanted her to explode like those volcanoes.

One, two, three fingers inside her sleek, tight wetness, while my thumb ground against her hard clit. With another woman, in another place, I would have wanted to lay her out, lick and tease and explore, but with Evie, right here and right now, I wanted to feel her come.

I wanted to make her come.

When she did, pulsing and undulating around my fingers, I swallowed her screams in a kiss. My own clit shivered in empathy, not quite an orgasm but with the same rhythmic throbbing as Evie's climax.

She fumbled down and stroked me, and I shuddered and rocked against her fingers, pressing my face against her collarbone and begging for mercy.

She gasped about not having a roommate, which was all I really needed to hear. (Jeanne was a dear friend, but I wanted time alone with Evie: wanted, desired, needed, required, would murder for.)

Tomorrow we'd surf. Tomorrow, maybe we'd talk about the future, if there was any sort of future to talk about.

Tonight, though, was about being lost in the tropics with Evie.

CANVAS

Kenzie Mayer

'm in the bathroom, my wrists going numb from the handcuffs. Every few minutes, I stand on my tiptoes. It relieves
the strain some, and then the pins and needles come. Numb's
better. They're in the living room laughing and talking, watching
videos. Her friends have been here for hours. I don't know if
they know I'm in here.

I know it's pretty bad and I'd laugh if it weren't happening to
me...but I can't remember her name. Honestly, she's a complete
stranger. I don't even remember picking her up...or being picked
up, and that's usually my favorite part. I love the game of pred-
ator and prey. I like being wanted. I like the pain of wanting. I
love seduction. I love the act of devouring, surrendering.

I woke up here in the bathroom, and I've been waiting ever
since. I could probably shove the gag out with my tongue, work
it down my chin and scream. The gag's loose and wet from my
saliva and tears, but my mouth is dry and I'm afraid to move
my tongue. There's blood on the floor, and I don't think all of it

came from her piercing my nipples. My back throbs and when I move, things tear back there, and I bleed some more.

Most of all, I don't know if her friends will help me or hurt me more.

I can't remember how I got here. I can't remember what I was doing before waking up here in the bathroom, handcuffed to the link in the ceiling.

The footsteps tell me that she's not the only one coming back into the bathroom. I sob, muffled in the limp gag. The doorknob turns. My eyes close. I'm terrified. I don't know if I'm going to live through this. They could do whatever they wanted with me.

I'm dripping wet. I honestly can't wait.

My hands are covered in paint. I love the feel of paint. Thick fat silk, cold at first, warmed quickly. I always want to shove my hands in my mouth and drink it down. I always want to roll in it, drown in it. When I go see other artist's shows, I worship their brushstrokes, their thick layers of color, the shape of light, the forms of shadow.

I once got kicked out of the Metropolitan Museum for licking the glass that protected one of Goya's black book paintings. When Ralph Fiennes ate the William Blake painting in *Red Dragon*, I laughed and laughed. I understood completely.

It's not enough to touch paint, to caress it. I want it on the inside moving within me like a living creature. I want it on my tongue, thick as chocolate, smelling like musk and incense. I want it in my blood, burning pathways in my veins.

I love having sex in paint. Amy says I'm making love to the paint, though, not her. She asks if I even need her to be there, 'cause it doesn't seem like it. She teases and asks if I even remember her name, says it isn't cerulean blue. It's not alizarian crimson either or azo yellow.

I look up. The canvas stretches across the entire wall. I don't remember stretching this. I'd have to, 'cos canvas this big costs a bloody fortune. It's my painting, too. I've already started on it. My signature style: thick paint plastered on with my fingers, arbitrary color straight from the tube, curvy sensuous lines implying movement and breath. I want my paintings to live. Death terrifies me: stillness without end. I'm afraid if I stop moving, I won't be able to breathe. Sharks never stop moving. They swim and hunt in their sleep.

I walk around and pull the canvas edge forward. I didn't stretch this. This canvas was professionally done. I can't afford this. How the hell did I get it?

"Amy." Louder. "Amy."

I come back around the side of the canvas, nearly stepping on tubes of paint. I stop and stare. Panic rises. There's a lot of paint on the floor. Most of the tubes are still in boxes. There're cans of paint, too. Did I go crazy and buy out the store? Amy's going to kill me. I probably used her credit cards. Okay, I *know* I must have used her credit cards. I don't have any money. Hell, I barely can keep a real job…selling paintings is all I've got going. I can't even afford this house alone. Without Amy I don't have a damned thing….

"AMY!"

"Yeah?" She leans against the door, soup bowl of coffee cradled in her hands. She watches me, dark hair framing her foxlike face, her smile mysterious: Japanese Fox Princess. I can't remember what it means for the heroes in the folktales when a Japanese Fox Princess falls in love with them. I remember though, strangely enough, that in the Irish/Scottish tales, the Selkie Wife leaves the Husband Hero who hurts her. Or is that when he returns her skin?

"Amy." I spread my paint-smeared hands, indicating the canvas, the paint. Caught red-handed! "I think I screwed up."

She nods and the smile never leaves her mouth. Something's off though. I smile back, trying to win her. Do Japanese Fox Wives go samurai kamikaze on their lovers? Do Selkie Wives eat their wayward husbands?

"Yes," Amy says, turning away, "you did."

I know what's off. Amy's smile never reaches her dark almond eyes.

I'm naked, and except for the candles on the floor lighting the way, it's dark. My instructions are to crawl to them, even though the double-headed dildo is brushing the floor with every step and shoving deep inside me, even though the tickler part strokes my clitoris and I want to press down harder. I must crawl *slowly* on my hands and knees and *not* give in before I get to the bed. If I come to them too quickly, they will make me start all over again.

I know this for a fact 'cause I woke up here an hour ago...and I've been crawling ever since.

The last time I got to them, to the side of the bed, the blonde reached down and felt me. I knelt before her, sitting back on my heels, my thighs spread. The other end of the dildo was on the floor. It took all of my strength not to push into it. Inside, I was greedy, hungry, pulling at the dildo. But I sat my cunt at the edge of it, the edge of the cliff. I will not jump.

The wetness on my thighs was warm, and I was purring. The blonde adjusted the strap on the double head. The rocking of it inside me made me moan. She put her fingers in my mouth. I tasted me, some of her. She'd gotten wet watching me crawl down the candlelit hall. The slight taste of both of us rocked my hips. Her girlfriend, a petite redhead, moved to rest her head on the blonde's hip. She licked her lips like a cat observing a bird with a broken wing.

"Stop," the blonde whispered. "If you come before us, there will be punishment."

"What kind of punishment?"

My voice came out husky, hoarse. Was the punishment going to be that I lick them clean? Was the punishment being used over and over again like a tool, a machine, my tongue and lips working endlessly as I sang into their nether lips, my fingers warm as bees in their honey? The dildo moved slick and fast between us, the sound of it slapping against flesh. There was hunger, hunger in our breath, in our hands. Was the punishment going to be another hour of crawling on my hands and knees before them, so wet I was actually swooning?

Or was the punishment being tossed out...throbbing like this, nearly mad with need?

The petite redhead murmured into her girlfriend's belly, "She said we could do anything we want."

Had I said that? When? I couldn't remember anything past an hour ago. I couldn't even remember coming here.

"Yes," I agree now, my voice a ghost, pale in the dark, disappearing. "Whatever you want. I'll do whatever you want."

The redhead reaches over and gently tugs at my nipple. She twists it and I cry out, thrusting into the dildo. I stop myself from going too much farther, shaking. The redhead laughs. She crawls up closer to my face, her pale soft breasts now sitting in the blonde's lap. Her tongue flicks out, snakelike, catching the tip of my nose, the side of my cheek. I lean into her, eyes closing. I lick my lips, starving.

She whispers, her breath stirring against my face, "You don't even know our names, do you?"

I really don't. But, to be fair...I can barely remember my own name right now. I shake my head no. I can't stop trembling.

"She's bad. We should make her earn our forgiveness." The

redhead pulls back and sits up. "And you'll do anything to make us forgive you, won't you?"

Yes. I really will.

"No matter how humiliating. How degrading."

I stare at her. I don't mean to, but I start crying. I could be somewhere nice right now with my girlfriend. I could be making slow love to her, showing her everything I can never say. I could be telling her things about me, about my past, asking for acceptance and then...taking that acceptance, appreciating the fact that someone knew things about me and still liked me. It would be easy. But, instead, it was so damned hard.

I wipe my face with the back of my hand. I whisper, "Yeah, no matter what. I can take whatever you got." I win this. This is what I do. I'm good at this. And you can't beat me 'cause no matter how awful it is, I will always survive. I will always burn clean.

The redhead laughs again. She pushes herself to the edge of the bed, shoving her cunt into my face. She spreads her wet lips with her fingers. Even in the dim light of the candles, she shines like a string of pearls, like dew before a storm. The musk of her reaches me. It's a heady scent. I can nearly taste her, based on that smell alone. I moan.

"I have to pee a little. Beg to drink me. Then, beg again to eat me."

I beg.

This painting is...it's brought me to my knees. When the hell did I do that? How did it come out of me? Ripping, tearing...did my soul scream out when it broke away from me? I step back. I don't know if I can ever do anything like this again. I'm suddenly terrified. What if I can't? Now that I've tasted it...it's all I want. I want to paint like this...live in this always. Everything else tastes like ashes in my mouth.

Amy comes up behind me, wrapping her arms around me. I feel suffocated. I wriggle anxiously. Amy lets me go, steps back. Quietly, she says, "I brought you something to drink. It will... help you work."

Amy puts the mug in my hand. I can't take my eyes off the painting. I drink blindly, barely tasting it.

"Do you see?" I whisper.

"Yes," Amy says, "I do see."

I think it's a blindfold...no, it's heavier than that...a mask? I'm nude and bound. The hands spin me, touch my breasts, my belly; stroke my thighs; glance off my shoulders. Dizzy, I feel like giggling but there's a rubber ball in my mouth. Vertigo. Vortex. Suddenly I stop. A hand steadies me, pulling on the ball gag in my mouth. I rock in space. My arms and legs are tied up behind me. Only the ropes, the ties that connect me to the ceiling, hold me in place. I'm cold where the binding ties don't cover me. My nipples stand erect, the chain tinkling lightly as I sway in the ropes.

Fingers pull at my nipples, jerk at the chain that connects them. They tickle my breasts, my belly. I moan. Fingers probe my cunt, slipping in wetly, pulling out smoothly. The sound of it is like a mouth suckling...I jerk into their hands, hips thrusting against air. I hear laughter. There are a few women here, their laughter like bells, like song.

The hands move, slide into the crevice of my ass, twist easily into the hole, my juice a lubricant. Then there's a mouth at my nether lips, a tongue stroking my inner walls, teeth nibbling at the outer lips. I come *undone*, nearly tearing myself free of the bindings like a bird caught in a spiderweb. There's more laughter and then coldness as the hands withdraw. I sob, chewing down on the rubber ball, nearly panting with need.

A voice at my ear says, "Do you know who I am?"

I shake my head no.

"Do you care?"

I hesitate. No, I don't care. I really don't care. But is it safe to admit that?

"Answer me truthfully. No matter what that truth is. Tell me the truth and I will suck you raw. I will make you scream. I will fuck you until you are good and broken. And then, I will give you to the others." She waits. Then, "Do you care who I am?"

I shake my head no.

"Do you give me permission?"

Yesssssss.

I wake up worn out, exhausted, but I don't know why. It's a struggle to sit up. I'm on the floor in the studio and the last canvas stands before me, finished, wet, but done. The others line the walls. I must have twenty...maybe fifty paintings here, easily enough for a show. It's been a long time since I've done this much work, this quickly. And they're good. I can feel that. I don't fool myself when it comes to that. I'm a harsh judge...I know when I finally get it right.

I've given it everything I've got, and I don't know if I have anything left for me.

Oh, sweet demons are now exorcised for they have had their way with me. Amen. Blessed be. Praise Allah. Jackie the agent will dance happily and sanity is restored to the universe. I don't remember painting all of them, though. I remember a lot of black space...blackout time. I remember parts of them...fragments of working, waking to see them finished, waking up and knowing where to put the next line, hearing the next color...

I must have passed out here and there, then. I do that. I get to working, I lose all track of time. If it weren't for Amy feeding me, forcing me to go to bed, I'd starve or die from exhaustion. Outside the window, it's that funny twilight that could mean early morning or early afternoon, that in-between time. Photographers call it the magic hour 'cause the light is soft and surreal. Photographs taken then are always perfect, moments trapped and sealed like treasures. It's the time I aim for when I take photos for the paintings.

I smell like last week's clothes. When did I last take a bath? I stand up and then, Jesus wept! I'm on my knees. What the hell? Everything hurts.

I reach behind me to feel my back. I can barely reach there without pain screaming up and down my body. There are scratches, long raised welts. Sobbing, I raise up my shirt. My breasts hurt and for a damn good reason. I have nipple rings on each breast, connected by a long delicate silver chain. So much for me nursing a baby. Amy was the one who wanted the family anyway. Even worse, my cunt feels like I've broken it. Well, if anyone can break her cunt.

When did all this happen? My head hurts just thinking about it. I get some flashes...memory comes in bits and pieces. I remember women and me doing things, having things done to me, and then there were times with Amy, here in the studio. But there's a lot, *a lot* of blackout time in there, too. I want to cry and then...

I look at the final canvas. I gotta say, if I didn't know me, I'd want to fuck me.

I laugh 'cause even if none of my work sells, I'll still be in love with it. With me. And now I can make love to my girl. "AMY!"

I wait a minute. Then I call out again. There's movement this time in the house, and Amy comes to the door. She's perfectly made up. Perfect little china doll, delicate and dangerous. Her dark almond eyes are puffy, eyeliner clinging to them wetly. Her mouth, though, is a bright red, angry pout, its mind made up. She's wearing her vintage Victorian traveling clothes. Amy spends a fortune on her clothes. She's so goth princess. I wear my Salvation Army threads till the patches won't hold them on me anymore...and then for some time after that. Amy calls it starving art-gypsy.

She says, "So it's done. You have enough for the show. Are you happy?"

"Uh, *yeah*. Aren't you? What's going on with the look? Are you a superspy now?"

Amy laughs. "Superspy. Ironic."

I laugh, too, but I really don't get it. I'm dumb on girl innuendo. I need stuff spelled out and then sounded out slowly, maybe even repeated. Tears well up in Amy's eyes. Angrily, she wipes at them. "God, you're...stupid. Unbelievable. Jesus..."

I wait. Frozen. How does it go? Animals freeze, flee or fight?

Amy bursts out, "You fucked all of them and didn't even stop to think, to question it." She sobs like something's breaking inside her. "You let them do whatever they wanted 'cause that's what you wanted."

I still can't move. Things hurt a hell of a lot all over my body. I may be paralyzed but I can still feel. Don't amputees feel phantom pains in their missing limbs?

Numb, I get out, "I don't know what you're talking about. I don't understand."

"No," Amy says, nodding angrily, "you really don't understand. Here's a map, genius. I know about the cheating. But I still couldn't leave you. I wanted you to love me back like I loved you. I wanted you to see what you were missing out on. So, I taught you a lesson." Amy waves her arms at the studio, at my paintings.

I shrug. I still don't get it. Amy screams at me, "I didn't pay for the canvas or paint, you did! I drugged you and sold you to my friends! I kept hoping you'd wake up, a *decent* human being would, wake up and make it stop! Stop fucking everything in sight!"

Oh. Oh, god. I sit down right there. I have flashes of more memory. She sold me. She drugged me and gave me to her friends, to teach me a lesson on intimacy.

Amy shakes, still standing in front of me. She no longer sees me, though. Rage has taken over. "Christ! I'm so stupid! I wasted time on you and you're just a whore! I actually loved you! And you will always be a whore!"

I cover my ears with my hands. I mumble, calming myself, soothing myself, "I just wanted to paint. I don't care about the rest. I just want to paint."

Amy settles dangerously low and quiet. The rage simmers. "Yes, that's right," she snarls. "It's all about you and what you want. Nothing else matters. No one else matters. It's all a mirror." Amy pulls in closer to me. I draw up inside myself, I withdraw, I flee! She whispers, whip sharp, "But you can't let anyone in 'cause there's nothing left inside you to see."

"Why did you do this?"

"Why did you?" Amy's crying again. I'm useless with tears. I don't know what to do. "All you had to do was love me back and it would have ended, it would have been like a dream. But you can't love anyone."

And she walked away. She moved her things out of our house.

I took the paintings to Jackie the agent. She found me a show in one of those avant-garde galleries downtown. It was a big deal. Jackie the agent earned her commission. She invited the press and some serious collectors for the opening. The owner of the gallery wore her dark hair in pigtails although she was closer to fifty than she was eleven. It suited her. She had a New York air about her. I wondered what she tasted like. I couldn't stop thinking about it.

Hung up, my work looked like bodies drained of blood, carcasses, Bluebeard's wives. How many women did he kill before a woman and her brothers killed him? Three? Seven? I don't remember. Many paintings sold. The ones that didn't... well, I didn't want to sell them anyway.

A lot of women came to the show. Some brought men, some came with other women. Some came alone. It didn't matter. I couldn't look any of them in the face. I have the smell of them on my fingers. I have the scent of them on my skin. I have them buried in my canvas.

THE ANGEL CONNECTION

C. B. Potts

M s. Drayborn." M'Linda's voice held equal measures of surprise and dismay. "I never expected you to come down here!"

Corrine smiled, hoping to put the big woman at ease. New entrepreneurs were always so nervous. "It's something we do with all the ventures we're seriously considering, M'Linda." She smiled. "The Angel Connection's never invested in a garage before, so I thought I'd come over and check out your shop for myself."

M'Linda smiled, the expression deepening as she realized the full impact of Corrine's words. "And you're more than welcome, Ms. Drayborn. That's for sure." She looked Corrine up and down. "Come on in. But you'll be wanting to be careful with them shoes, mind. OSHA's got us all in steel toes for a reason."

"I'll be careful." Corrine looked down at her shoes. They were Ferragamos and had set her back a cool four hundred dollars. "I always am."

It may have been the first garage Corrine had toured as a venture capitalist, but it was hardly the first one she'd set foot in.

M'Linda ran a tight ship. That was clear. Tools were neatly hung on pegboard racks or stowed in gleaming toolboxes. Air hoses were coiled in tight serpentine loops against the wall, rubbery reptilian red ringed round with caution yellow.

There was a car up on the lift. Two of M'Linda's Good Girl Garage all-female crew were peering up into its underbelly, obviously finding something noteworthy there.

A pickup truck occupied the other bay, battered and blue. A pair of legs stuck out from underneath on the driver's side, a few inches past the door frame. Legs that were wearing black jeans and the smallest steel-toed boots Corrine had ever seen.

Corrine squatted down next to the legs. "What're you working on?"

"Catalytic converter." The voice was young, pitched low. "It failed the emissions test first time round. I figure this'll get it through." Small hands gripped the edge of the frame and pulled the creeper forward. "Who wants to know?"

Corrine was looking into the brightest brown eyes she'd ever seen, in the middle of an incredibly young face. Spiky black hair fringed round a well-shaped skull, the shop lights glinting over the slick gel that'd pushed normally straight hair upward.

"I'm Corrine Drayborn, from the Angel Connection Investors' group. We're checking out M'Linda's shop."

"You're gonna buy M'Linda's place?" A charcoal eyebrow, no thicker than a thought, cocked upward. "I didn't know she was planning to sell."

"No." A small silver ring was set in the corner of this girl's nose, one that had three perfect matches in the upper curving arch of her ear. "Invest in it. Help her get it going the way she wants to."

"Hmm." The mechanic sat up on the creeper, running two petite hands over the front of her jeans. "I'm Kim Choi." She extended her hand. "Pleased to meet you."

A handshake should be a simple thing. Two palms meet, fingers clasp, a brief, joined motion and a parting. It happens a million times a day, all across the planet, and nothing comes of it.

But that was before Corrine and Kim shook hands. The first touch of flesh—smooth fingers meeting calloused counterparts—and Corrine knew it wouldn't be their last.

From the spark in Kim's eyes, that lightning-quick flash of recognition, Kim knew it too.

At least that's what Corrine told herself, desperate not to read too much into the mechanic's next words.

"So what can I do for you?"

In a brief, blinding moment, Corrine had a clear picture of exactly what Kim could do for her—what her trembling fingers would feel like as they unbuttoned that oil-stained work shirt, hovering in that strange point between reverence and eagerness to get to the slim frame below. Her ears echoed with the sure knowledge of how that heavy black leather belt that encircled Kim's slim waist would sound thudding to the floor. Her flesh burned with the surety of what that spiky hair would feel like against her thighs. It was a breathtaking moment.

"Um," she said, feeling the subtle burn of heat rising up the back of her neck. "Well, uh, tell me about M'Linda," she said, thick words tripping over a normally articulate tongue. "Is she a good boss?"

Kim smiled, knowing. "M'Linda's good people. She gave me a chance back when I first got out of school. Not many people would." She tilted her head toward the pickup. "Been working for her for two years now. Haven't met the vehicle I can't fix yet."

"So she's fair?" A pause, not nearly long enough. "A good boss?"

"I'd say so." Kim nodded. "And she's smart. Careful with what she buys, but makes sure we've got what we need. That's a good thing."

"Yeah," Corinne agreed, her attention captured by the faint shadow the neckline of Kim's uniform cast upon her flesh. "It is..."

Her words trailed away, leaving Corrine alone in the startled realization that she was blatantly checking out a woman young enough to be her daughter. That subtle burn of embarrassment she'd felt earlier became an inferno of mortification. Her cheeks were blazing, she was sure, bright red beacons that could be seen from space.

"Is there anything else you wanted?" Kim asked, her tone soft. "Ma'am?"

"You have a good relationship with her?" The words were out of Corrine's mouth before she could stop them. It took every ounce of willpower to keep her hands from flying to her face, fluttering fingers desperate to flatten over her mouth and stop their owner from revealing herself further. "As a boss, I mean."

"She's a very good boss." Kim's gaze was disconcertingly direct. "No one could ask for more." Her voice dropped just a fraction, rendering her words barely audible in the busy shop. "And I haven't."

"That's good, then." Corrine's hand slid into her jacket pocket, as she fumbled to regain her composure. "If you think of anything else, give me a call." She handed over a card, careful to avoid any more contact. It might render her completely incoherent. "Anytime."

"Thanks." Kim looked at the card and pushed it into her

shirt pocket. "Nice talking to you."

A little push of booted heels against the concrete, and she disappeared back under the truck.

"Likewise," Corrine said, turning toward the door. "Likewise."

Three deep breaths, and Corrine managed to pull it together. She looked over the rest of the Good Girl Garage with a calm and critical eye, taking the time to have much less…troubling… conversations with two of the other mechanics. Satisfied that all was as it had been described, she left, pausing in the front doorway to leave M'Linda with a final bit of reassurance.

"I don't see any problems, really. It's a very professional shop, and I can tell your team takes pride in what they do. We'll double-check the numbers one more time, but I don't foresee a problem. Everything looks good." Corrine looked up to discover Kim watching from the shadowy interior of the garage. "Really, really good."

Stupid, stupid, stupid. Corrine stalked through the living room, scotch in hand, to glare at the telephone that refused to ring.

It remained obstinately silent.

"I'm old enough to be her mother." She glared out her window, where the very last of the commuters were making their way home. "Little girl like that? She's not going to call me."

A red motorcycle sped by, the rider flattened over the gas tank. It wavered a bit as it wove around slower moving vehicles, angling toward the pavement with a reckless disregard of gravity.

"Idiot," Corrine muttered. "Get your fool self killed, riding like that."

The bike had barely reached the corner when the rider slowed, planted one tiny booted foot and yanked the bike around.

One really tiny booted foot. The smallest foot Corrine had ever seen.

"Oh, my." Moving much slower, the bike progressed back down the street, until the front tire nosed into a narrow space directly opposite Corrine's building. "Oh, my, oh, my, oh, my."

The knock was confident. Assured.

Corrine pulled the door open. "Kim."

Kim smiled. "You know you didn't want me to call." The door clicked shut behind her. "What we got to do, we can't do over no phone."

"What's that, Kim?" She'd not had that much scotch, but her tongue was still thick and awkward. Each syllable came hard. "What do we have to do?"

"For starters, this." Kim went up on tiptoe, sliding leather-clad arms around Corrine's neck. The kiss was bright and sharp and intense—chromed metal edges and a most demanding tongue; it was everything Corrine had expected and more. "You think I couldn't tell you wanted me?"

"You could tell?"

"A blind man could tell." Kim's teeth worried at the side of Corrine's neck, pulled into a perfect curving bow by the short, tough fingers twining through her hair. "I didn't have to see it. I could smell it."

Corrine blushed scarlet.

Kim laughed. "Don't be embarrassed. It's good to know what you want." Her fingers encircled Corrine's wrist and pulled it downward. "To show your desire."

There was a stiff hard bulge in the front of Kim's pants, unyielding and unsurprising all at the same time.

Blue eyes flickered to brown.

Kim smiled. "When I want something, I don't hide it."

"You can be bold," Corrine replied, "when you're young."

"You're not so old." A strong hand slid over the front of Corrine's blouse, cupping a breast. "Far as I can tell from these."

"And you would know?" A little note of teasing banter, just enough to cover the little gasp of pleasure contact brought.

"I would." Those fingers, knowing, tightened, just a bit, in just the right place. "Well enough."

"God, Kim." There was another kiss, deeper, more demanding. "What are you doing to me?"

"Only what you want, pretty lady." This kiss stole the air from Corrine's lungs. "Only what you want."

Only what you want had Corinne on her knees, fingers scrabbling over Kim's belt.

The cock revealed was firm and thick and bright, bright blue.

"I'd heard of blue balls," Corinne said, looking up with a giggle, "but this is a first."

Kim's fingertips were featherlight on her cheek. "Just want you to remember that I'm a boi, not a boy." A little waggle of the hips then, just enough to bring the head of the plastic shaft slowly toward Corrine's mouth. "I don't want anyone getting confused."

"I don't think there's any danger of that." Kim's hips were silken under Corrine's fingers, her ass surprisingly muscular.

"Mmm." Kim's hands were in her hair, pulling just enough. "Get me ready for you."

Logically, there should be no way for Corrine's mouth on a plastic shaft to give Kim pleasure. Strap-ons don't come with nerve endings installed, not even the best ones.

That didn't stop Kim from enjoying herself tremendously.

"That's it, pretty lady," she purred, slowly sliding past Corrine's lips. "You look so hot doing that, down there on your knees for me."

Corrine's hand dropped to her own nether regions.

Kim chuckled. "You want to touch yourself? That little pussy getting all hot for your boi?" She stepped backward, withdrawing herself. "I bet it is."

Corrine got to her feet, half-nodding as she rose.

"And you want your boi to take care of that for you?"

"Yeah." Corrine forced her eyes up. "I do. Ever since I saw you." Dealing with Kim was like dancing with a hurricane, she realized. Somehow she had to get some control of this situation, if only for a moment. "I had to have you."

"You will have me." Two steps, three steps forward, until Corrine was backed against the wall. "You'll have me inside you, soon enough."

Pants down, legs up—it was a dance as old as time, twisted somehow. Twisted by this spiky-haired girl who was nipping at her breasts—this girl who was strong enough to hold her in place with words and looks and well-timed caresses.

Corrine's palms were flat against the wall, fingers scrabbling over the smooth surface for purchase.

"Oh, my god."

Kim smiled, shifting her hips a fraction. Her legs were so soft against Corrine's thighs, flesh sliding silklike against itself, the friction a high counterpoint to a more demanding, primitive rhythm.

"You're so beautiful." She had two hands on Corrine's waist now, just enough to steady her while she came. "I love girls like you. All fancy in your suits and high heels."

Corrine's response was less than articulate, more moan than vocabulary.

"That's right. Give it up for your boi."

After, when thought returned to her head and air to her lungs, Corrine reached for Kim.

"Uh-uh." Narrow back turned toward her, Kim hitched her jeans closed. "Not yet." She reached for her motorcycle jacket, the leather shell adding another layer of armor to their communication.

"What do you mean, not yet?" Words came easier now, faster. "We just..."

"And we will again." Kim turned and went up on tip toe again, depositing a featherlight kiss on Corrine's forehead. "Maybe." She smiled. "We'll see after you make the decision about M'Linda's place."

And then she was gone, leaving Corinne staring at the door.

"Ms. Dearborn, how nice of you to stop by!" M'Linda greeted Corrine with a huge smile. "We've made some real improvements with the Angel money, and I'd love to show them to you."

"That would be great, M'Linda." Corrine followed the tall woman into the back of the garage and took in the new tire balancer, engine hoist and pipe bender. "And I see you've got some new faces around here, too."

One face was markedly absent. Kim was nowhere to be seen.

"Had to." M'Linda shrugged. "One of the girls is pregnant, and Doc put her on bed rest. She'll be back, I'm hoping, after her little boy is born. And Kim—the one you talked to last time? —wigged out on me. I haven't seen her in weeks."

"I hope I didn't scare her off," Corrine said. "Good mechanics are hard to find."

"I'm sure it wasn't you," M'Linda said. "Kim's a good girl, but she's got wandering feet." She shook her head. "You give these kids a chance and look what happens. I should have known better."

"You never know, do you?" Corrine asked. "Which ones

are going to stay around?" It was her turn to shake her head. "When they're young like that."

"The good ones always go."

Outside, a red motorcycle went by, slowly. Very slowly. Corrine turned, just in time to catch a glimpse of the rider peering into the garage's interior. She smiled.

"Not always, no."

A STORY ABOUT SARAH

Cheyenne Blue

They tell you that when you start writing things down, you should write about what you know and what you love. When my head was so full of stories that I had to let some loose, I started with those that were easiest to tell.

What do I know: I know how to sing. I know how to cook. I know how the land smells after the rain that rarely falls. I know how to stop a child's tears although I've no kids of my own. I know how to gentle a skittish colt so that he follows me around like a dog. And I know Sarah.

What do I love: I love this land; I love its silence and its emptiness. I love the red rocks that jumble along the creek. I love the gargle of magpies in the morning. I love how under my hands food comes together to make a meal. And I love Sarah.

This is a story about Sarah. It's the first story that fell out of my head, but stories about Sarah are as many and winding as the tracks on a scribbly gum.

My name is Melly and I'm forty-four years old. I'm half

Yamatji and half white. The Yamatji half came from the desert in Western Australia where I sometimes go; the white half came from Germany where I've never been. My Yamatji mother died when I was little, or maybe she went outback. I like to think of her roaming the land, digging for grubs, knowing where to find food, living the old way. Maybe she died of drink, but I don't want to know if she did.

I cook for the workers here at the mining camp where I live. I got the job when I was fifteen. My German pa worked at the camp, and we lived here as well. Most of the kids wanted to leave; they wanted to go to Perth, or to the shore where the waves curled. Not me. I wanted to stay in this sunburned little settlement. So I took the first job that was offered.

I met Sarah when I was sixteen and she was a year older. She also worked at the camp, in the office. Her pa was the mine manager, and Sarah used to do something with books and paper. We were the only two girls there, so it was natural that we'd hang together. Sarah never minded the color of my skin. It mattered to people then; it doesn't now.

Sarah was slender, back when we were girls. She was skinny, with knees that were the widest part of her legs and a chest like a boy's. She had long curly brown hair that fell nearly to her waist. She wore it in a thick plait down her back, all crinkly and barely contained. Now she's sturdy and wide, and she has breasts that are ample and spreading. Her hair is still thick and curly, but now there's gray in it, and it's short and hugs her head. That's Sarah.

The boys at the mine all wanted to take Sarah out, but her pa kept a strict eye on her. The boys didn't want to take me out, at least not where we would be seen. And I didn't want to go with them anyway. Instead, Sarah and I would go places together: down to the billabong to swim, up the wallaby path to the top of the rocks where we'd sit and look out over the camp. Sometimes we'd spy on the men and giggle. More often, we'd sit in the shade of a scribbly gum and talk.

This is a story about Sarah, but it's also a story about Sarah and me. Sarah and me together.

She kissed me the first time. I kissed her back the second time. The times after that, I don't remember. We weren't girls then; I was twenty, she the year older. And then we were lovers.

We'd do our loving outdoors, always in the open, never in my room at the camp or at her pa's house. We'd climb to the top of the rocks, where there was a hidden place. The red sand was soft, and there was patchy shade when the sun was low. Best of all, you'd never guess it was there, not unless you happened over the rocks not following any path and stumbled across it. So we never worried about being caught. I'm not sure what would have happened if someone had found us, but it doesn't matter now. After our nearly thirty years together, most of them know and most of them don't care. Any that do care stay away.

We had a blanket that we stashed in a cranny in the rocks. We'd shake it out well, so that the spiders and sometimes a scorpion or little tiger snake were dislodged, and we'd spread it down on the sand. We'd take off our clothes immediately. There was no delicate disrobing, we'd just stand and undress. The red sand would spill over the edge of the blanket, and often our skins would be so wet with sweat that the sand would stick, coating us with marbled patterns of red. It seemed right to be naked there, out in the sun, out on the earth. Once we were undressed, we'd never put our clothes back on until it was time to walk home. Have you ever been naked under the sun? If you have, you'll never forget it.

Sometimes we still do our loving outdoors, although it's not as easy for us to climb the rocks to reach our place, and often we're too lazy.

This is a story about Sarah and how she kisses.

At first, we did nothing but kiss: gentle kisses, almost chaste. Sarah says that she wanted to make them into more, but she was afraid of what I'd do, what I'd say, how I'd laugh at her. But I wanted the same, and one day, suddenly, we were really kissing, tongues together, and there were wet lips and saliva and it was all very hot and desperate. I loved her kisses. I loved how her lips were so firm and how soft they would be if it weren't for the sand that coated them. There was an edge of pain from the way that the grains rubbed and ground into our lips. She'd stop, and wipe the sand from my lips and hers with a finger, but it was no good. It would be back again the next time.

It was a long time before we did anything but kiss. Months. Why seek more when what you have is so perfect? Sarah's kisses are like the creek that flows down the red bluff after rain: at first it's barely there, the merest hint of what's to come, before it swells and falls into something so deep you could drown in it. Then it overflows, and unleashed it swirls into a fierce, raging passion.

This is a story about Sarah and how she likes to be loved.

Sarah likes to be in charge. When we make love, she likes to direct how it will go. She leads my fingers to where she wants them on her body. I never mind, as I love her skin and I love to caress her, slowly if that's what she wants, so slowly that I think I can feel each pore, each grain of sand on her skin. I love to touch her breasts like that, circling around and around, a sort of aimless pattern that is not actually aimless at all, closer and closer to her nipple. Sarah's breasts were tiny and barely there once. Now they're ripe and full and lush, just as she is. When I stroke her like this, she wiggles like a black snake caught by the tail, twisting, trying to slide her body under my fingers if they won't move faster over her body.

"Mel-ly," she says, and my name is broken down into long pieces, each a part of the whole. Sometimes she just calls me Mel, and when she does, I think she's leaving part of me behind.

When my fingers finally find her nipple, she sighs, just once, as if she's come home. Maybe she has. Her nipples are sensitive and she doesn't like them treated roughly. So I worship them, stroking their dark peaks, as dark and red as desert flowers, and then I take one of them in my mouth and suckle gently, oh, so gently. She loves that, and her hands wind into my hair, not holding me there, just letting me know she likes what I'm doing.

Sarah lets me know when she wants more. If I touch her cunt before she wants it, she'll push my hand away, gently, not rudely, just telling me she's not quite ready. I stroke her waist while I'm waiting for her signal, the indent above her hips— once so narrow and boyish, now wider with padding that hides her bones. I kiss her tummy, tickling with my tongue to make her giggle or sigh, and I stroke her thighs, feeling for that special place on the inside where the skin is softest.

I can always smell her cunt. Sarah's smell is different from mine—and I have no one else to compare with. She smells musky and warm like fresh-baked bread, salty like the sea, sharp like bush lemons. When she's excited, her woman-smell surrounds her so that I can taste it on her skin, not only in her pussy.

When she wants me to touch her cunt, she takes my hand and pushes it down. Or she'll shift so that she's sitting and open her legs invitingly. I'll use my fingers to stroke, to circle her clit with the light touch she loves—too heavy and she'll flinch away. I'll push two, three fingers up inside her and I'll use my thumb to rub. My hands are as dexterous as a piano player's. She hums and I play.

I taste her. I eat her. I push my face up between her legs, so far that my nose is wedged against her mound, my chin wet with her juices. She smells so strong then, and I love it. I lick her delicately, using my tongue all around her pussy, pushing it inside and then around and around her clit. She's vocal, my Sarah, and she hums and sighs and grunts in pleasure. Sometimes she'll hold my head, trying to direct me, but I've been doing this for so long that I know the moves; I know the paths that she loves the most.

She shivers when she comes, a whole-body sort of shiver that starts at her toes, travels up along her legs, so tautly held, and into her rigid abdomen. She clenches down as if pushing herself into the blanket, into the red earth, will make her come harder. If my fingers are inside her, I can feel her internal little tremors too, all flickering and shivery. It would be a delicate dance around my fingers, except that she's so strong. She always comes; once, maybe twice.

This is a story about Sarah and how she loves.

Sarah likes to surprise, which is the opposite of how she likes me to love her. Sometimes she blindfolds me and leaves me lying there in the patterns of sunlight. I can barely breathe when she does that. I lie there waiting for her to touch me, wondering where it will be. Maybe she'll kiss me again, maybe she'll kiss my breast or my belly or the rise of my hip bone. Maybe she'll just spread my thighs and plunge her tongue into my cunt. Or maybe she'll brush me with a scratchy piece of bark or trickle hot sand onto my skin from a height, so that the grains pepper me like buckshot before forming their own little pyramid. Sometimes an insect will run over my skin and I won't know if it's her. That makes her laugh in delight.

Always though, Sarah likes to please.

"D'you like that?" she says, or, "That feel good?" Even when she knows the answer—which is most of the time after all our time together—she still likes to ask. And she catalogs my grunts and sighs and incoherent responses and works out the answer for herself.

Sarah likes to use her fingers more than her tongue, as then she can watch my face. She says I'm most beautiful when I come. I don't believe her, but I like to hear her say it anyway. So most of the time, she uses her fingers—three, four, sometimes her whole hand—and she pistons and thrusts and fucks me as hard as I can take. Her fingers are nimble and flexible; she knows my insides better than I do, and she knows where to press so that I come alive under her hand. She can make me wetter than the creek in no time at all, and the wetter I get, the more she likes it.

Afterward, when I've come so hard that my stomach muscles ache with the spasms, she cradles my head and strokes my hair from my face and croons to me.

This is a story about Sarah, and me and her together.

It's not just about her. It's not just me doing her, and it's not just about me either. It's give and take. We both know what we like and we share that giving. We know which one of us needs it first, needs it most. And afterward, we lie together on the bright blanket with the gray-green leaves overhead. The air is hot and dry, and our skins are hot and damp. Afterward, it's about patterns: the leaves above our heads, the movement of her breath on my skin, the ritual of our loving completed. If I close my eyes, the sun and shade are still there behind my eyelids and Sarah is there too. She's always there, in my head.

We get up and take turns brushing the sand from our bodies. Then we dress, putting on shorts and T-shirts, and we roll up the blanket and put it back in the nook in the rocks for the next time. Hand in hand, we wander back to our weatherboard house at the edge of the camp that we've shared for the last twenty-one years. It has a verandah that looks west, toward the ocean although the ocean is far, far away. Sarah and I sit on our big double rocker, drink a cold beer and watch the sunset. Sarah thinks of the ocean and how she'd like to feel the salt water surround her.

I think of Sarah and how I'd like to feel her surround me again.

This was a story of Sarah. Sarah and me. Together.

THE WEEKEND

Delilah Devlin

I placed the grocery bag on the counter, set down my purse, then glanced around the airy living room of the cabin. It was early Friday evening—the first night of a lovers' weekend I'd planned down to the last detail.

The view through the large picture window was of the small lake, the water shining without a single ripple to mar the mirror-like surface. A lone figure walked along the bank, hands thrust deep into pockets, while the rising wind tore at her pale hair.

I swallowed hard and hesitated. Did she want company? Did she need more time to think about us, about whether we still "worked"?

That's what this weekend was all about: a last chance to renew our connection. Or maybe this was good-bye. I could no longer read from her expression what went on inside her head.

I wiped my hands along the sides of my thighs and pushed open the glass door that opened onto steps to the path that wound to the narrow beach.

Kari didn't look my way as I approached. Her arms wrapped around her middle as she stared at the water. "No problem getting away?"

"No. I had the days."

"Good. Have you unpacked?" At last, she glanced my way. Something in her eyes gave me hope. For the first time in a long time, she met my gaze and really looked at me.

I smiled. "Not yet. But would you like a glass of wine before we get settled?"

"That and a fire. It's colder than I thought it would be." She stepped closer. Her arm settled at my waist and she leaned in to hug me from the side.

Kari was the kind to kiss friends on the lips or offer a tight hug, so I couldn't rely on the gesture to mean anything. I draped an arm around her waist, and we walked slowly back to the cabin.

Inside, the fire took me only minutes. I placed several logs and kindling in the grate and as soon as the crackling fire was built, the air inside the cabin lost its crisp edge. I pulled my sweater over my head, and, dressed only in a tank and my jeans, I sat cross-legged on the hearth rug.

A glass dangled in front of me. "Thanks," I murmured. "I was supposed to get that. Sorry."

She sat beside me. "This was a good idea. This weekend."

"Yeah." I didn't know what else to say, hoping she'd let me know what had been on her mind. We'd been so busy working, too tired and stretched to hook up, that we'd drifted apart. I didn't like feeling like I was in this alone—the only one worried that our relationship was on its last legs.

Friends had introduced us, knowing that both Kari and I had dated women before and knowing my preference for waiflike blondes. We shared a lot of the same interests, were close to the same age. I'd ended a long relationship and hadn't really wanted to fall directly into another, but I did want companionship.

We'd landed in bed together that same night, the attraction so hot and fast that it took my breath away. She was like that. A bolt of lightning not easily captured. Even from the start, I began preparing myself for it to end.

I must have stared at the fire too long. A kiss landed on my shoulder. A hand slipped beneath the hem of my tank and glided upward to cup a breast. Kari moved closer and her body snuggled against my back.

Again, that urgent desperation to connect filled me. I leaned away and drew the shirt over my head, then leaned back again, letting the fire warm my front, her supple body heat my back. I reached behind me and sank my fingers in her silky hair, waiting.

Lips trailed along my neck. "Wanna fuck?" she whispered and bit my earlobe.

I smiled, then shivered because her fingers plucked my nipple a little too hard. "So long as I get a taste and soon."

Soft laughter gusted against my skin, and she pulled away. I turned to watch as she stripped. She walked naked toward her backpack and drew out a long, thick dildo—one I hadn't seen before. "I've been saving this."

I lay on my back and shimmied out of my jeans and panties. Watching her rub the gel-shaft around her lips as she walked to me made me wonder again whether she was seeing anyone—someone with a set of balls, because she did love cock.

"Shall I?" I asked, rising on my elbows. Kari liked to be shafted while I sucked her clit.

"Later. I'm going to play first."

She pressed her heel into my shoulder and shoved me to my back. Then she placed her feet on either side of my hips and squatted. "You have been way too uptight lately."

"I've missed you."

"You missed this, don't you mean?" Her eyes narrowed into catlike slits. "Margot's a grumpy girl when she doesn't get some." She dropped the dildo on the rug and leaned over me, the change of angle rubbing her wet pussy against my mound.

The humid heat seeped into my skin; the scent of her, musky and pungent, lured my fingers down to play.

Kari groaned as I slid my thumb over her clit. "No fair. I'm supposed to be the one in charge."

"You are." I grinned. "I wouldn't be tempted if you would quit rubbing your pussy there."

Her laugh was sharp and pained. "*Fffuck!*" Her eyes closed and she jerked her hips forward and back, grinding her clit on my finger while her moisture dribbled through my own pulsing lips.

She gave one last sexy slide and then pushed down my body. "Did I ever tell you I love a bald pussy?"

"A time or two," I gasped. Two fingers stroked inside me, swirling and stretching my entrance. I cupped my breasts and began to rock my hips, trying to lure her deeper or seduce her into putting her mouth where I needed it most.

The flat of her tongue lapped the swelling folds. "I like it almost as much as I like you."

I glanced down and caught her gaze.

Her nose wrinkled. "I know I haven't been around much. I needed to think."

"You get things figured out?"

"Almost." Her fingers slid away and she reached for the dildo. She tucked the first four inches in her mouth and twirled it, then pulled it away. A string of spit, stretching from her lips to the tip of the soft lifelike cap, had me thinking for the first time that I might like to watch her going down on a man. She'd be insatiable. Her hungry little mouth would gobble him up and have him cramming deep into her throat.

"Yeah, hold that thought," she said, her expression smug.

"Now you can read my mind?"

"Your tits are spiking." Her wide mouth stretched. "You wanna see me do a dude."

"What I wanna see is you doing something with that dildo besides teasing me."

Her laughter tinkled. No other way to describe it or her. Kari was elflike—small, slender, her frame so narrow she looked like a prepubescent teen from the rear.

I was anything but petite. And I liked the fact I could subdue her with just my weight. Liked the way her eyes would darken when I rolled on top and began to pump my hips. Sometimes, I wore a strap-on, because I knew she liked it. But I'd left it at home, wanting nothing but our mouths and hands this weekend, nothing but ourselves.

I should have known she wouldn't leave home without one of her own toys.

The cock kicked to life, humming loudly. The first glide landed on my clit, and she held the dildo there until the vibrations made the sensitive knot swell. She pulled the toy away, bent and latched on to me with her lips and sucked, drawing hard twice, then releasing with a succulent pop.

My heartbeats slowed to a deep, rhythmic thrum. I raised my knees and planted my feet wide apart, opening to her, nestling into the furry rug at my back and resting my head on both my arms so that I could watch.

She stretched my folds and tugged them upward, then leaned closer so that I could feel the warm gusts of her shortening breaths against me. Her tongue trailed along the edges of the outer lips, up and down. The tip of the dildo pushed inside me, just past the flanged ridge surrounding the cap, but no deeper. The humming tantalized and a gentle convulsion rippled up my channel.

It wasn't enough, and I growled to tell her so.

A smile kicked up one corner of her mouth, and she twisted the cock inside me. My pussy clasped noisily around it, trying to trap it, but she pulled it out again.

I slipped one hand from under my head and thrust my fingers into her soft, straight hair, tugging hard to punish her.

"What do you want, Margot?" she asked, her voice filled with teasing laughter. "Gotta tell me. Gotta make me hot."

"Turn your ass around this way, and I'll make you hot." I'd wanted to sound surly, but I was panting too hard to be convincing.

"You'll get your turn. Promise. But if you want more, you've gotta give it to me dirty."

"Fuck. You expect me to be articulate when all I can think about is how fucking hot you look, lying between my legs?"

"There's a start." She raised an eyebrow, waiting...

I rolled my eyes and blew out a deep breath. "Okay...I want that plastic penis cramming up inside me and your mouth sucking my clit."

"Cramming? Like this?" She twisted it, gently screwing it into me, but only about three inches.

My pussy clenched around the shaft, trying to draw it deeper. Again, I growled, frustration making me grind my teeth.

Her lips were set in a straight line as though she were trying to keep from laughing.

"I want your hand cupping the fucking base of that plastic prick and you shoving it up until you're slapping my cunt. I want all of it, bitch."

Her lips pursed. Her hazel eyes narrowed. "Callin' me names, now? What if I don't like that?"

"You fucking love it. Fucking little whore. Fucking cunt."

Kari giggled and dove down, slurping as she sucked my clit and *crammed* the dildo deeper.

"That's it, bitch," I breathed. "Fuck, yeah. Bite it. Scrape it with your teeth."

I closed my eyes as she ratcheted up the heat, her mouth sliding over my clit, sucking, her tongue feathering over it, then, at last, her teeth chewing it, every scrape making my body writhe.

"Fucking talented. Oughta sell clit-jobs. Make a fucking fortune."

She snickered. "You know you talk like a dude when you get desperate."

"I know what the fuck I want," I said, pulling her hair again. "And you talk too much."

Her lips latched harder, and she shoved the whole six inches deep inside me, her hand sliding in the moisture she'd coaxed from inside me when it met my pussy.

My hips rose and fell; moans, one after the other, ripped from my throat. "Fuck, yeah. Fuck, *fuck*." And then the spiraling coil deep inside my belly loosened. I sucked in a deep breath and rode the high, clutching her head with both hands.

When my fingers slipped away, Kari withdrew the cock and turned it off. Then she crawled upward to rest on her side next to me. She caressed a breast, bending to kiss one of the hard little spikes. "You know we have to talk," she whispered.

I sighed. "Yeah, we do."

"I want more," she said quietly.

"More what?" The words came out flat, with a tinge of annoyance. I winced inside, but I don't take rejection well.

"More...company."

"You want to see other people?" I closed my eyes, bracing for it. I could do this. I could share her. I just didn't want to lose her completely. Maybe that made me weak, but I was falling for her.

"Do you?"

I peeked at her from beneath the fringe of my eyelashes, trying to gauge what her idle-sounding question really meant. If I said no, would she be afraid to be honest? But I didn't want to see anyone else. Kari with her spritelike body and small kitten face was the only one I wanted to hover over while I fucked her.

I gave her a cowardly shrug. My throat was too tight to push words out.

She blew out an exasperated breath. "Dammit, Margot. You aren't easy, are you?"

"How can you say that? Didn't you have my pants off an hour after we met?"

"Don't be smug. I'm serious. Things have to change."

I sat up and raked a hand through my hair, feeling frustrated and grumpy. "Can we table this until after I make you come?" Maybe if I proved to her that she wasn't going to get any better than me, she'd be satisfied. Or maybe she'd just forget about this conversation. I could keep her busy all weekend with my mouth and fingers, keep her turned inside out and fuck-fogged. Then maybe we could put off talking until she loved me as much as I loved her.

Her mouth twisted and her eyes filled. I bent quickly and kissed her, cupping her head and taking her mouth gently. "Don't you cry," I said harshly when I pulled back.

Her mouth crimped tighter.

I shoved her to her back and crawled on top, trapping her legs between mine, wrapping my hands around her wrists and pinning her to the floor. "This is good. What we have could be fucking great."

She made a noise, but I didn't want to hear a protest, and I covered her mouth again, eating her lips the way I wanted to eat her pussy. "Just shut up. Talk later. Told you, I wanna taste."

When I came up for air, she whispered, "Sometimes, you're such a bitch."

"Who's talking dirty now?"

I scooted downward, hovering over one breast. Her nipples were softer than mine, velvety, puffy little cones—pale peach and just a shade or two darker than the soft skin surrounding them. "You've got the prettiest tits I've ever seen."

"If you like them B-B sized," she groused.

"I do. Aren't you lucky?"

She snorted, but she settled deeper against the carpet.

I had her now. I ignored the dildo and buried my face between her legs, sucking on her outer lips, sinking my tongue between them to catch the tangy fluid seeping from inside her.

I thrust two fingers into her pussy and thumbed her clit, rasping my thumb over the hard, rounded knot.

Tremors shook the thighs tightening around me and made her belly jump. Her head thrashed, her eyes squeezed shut.

I worked two more fingers inside, cupping them to make them fit, and began the rhythmic push-pull while I bent closer and swirled my tongue over her clit, which had swelled past its hood.

She came hard, jerking up her hips. I suctioned harder, pulling with my lips until she let loose a breathless, choked scream and settled again.

Her fingers threaded through my hair and tugged, and I moved up her body, covering her. Resting on my elbows, I cupped her face and kissed her.

When I broke the kiss, I framed her face with my palms. "I don't want anyone but you. But if you need more, if you aren't ready for it to be just about you and me, I'll wait until you're sure. I won't push."

Her eyes glittered and her arms wrapped around me. "I was going to ask you if I could move in with you. My lease is up. I need to make plans."

I held still, trying not to get too excited. "You're welcome to live with me. You can take my office—"

Kari pressed a finger to my lips. "Shut up. I'll be straight. I don't know if I'll never want anyone else again. But I'd like that to be *our* decision, because I'm with you. We aren't going to be roommates. I plan to sleep in your bed."

The tightness in my chest that I hadn't been aware of until that moment eased. I grinned down at her, watched her expression soften, watched her flick her tongue around her mouth and knew she wanted me to kiss her again.

It was enough for now. More than I'd hoped for when I arrived. "And to think we still have two more days...."

LOVE AND DEVOTION

Jove Belle

The crunch-slide of tires on gravel is my twenty-second warning that I'm about to have company. If I had enough time, I would strip and answer the door naked. As it stands, I barely have time to check my teeth for signs of the pizza I'd been eating and run my hands through my hair. Lonnie slams through the door, leaving a string of *fucking hells* and *damnations* in her wake.

"Lon, what's going on?" I sound like I'm not happy to see her, which isn't true. I'm mostly just not happy to see her car—a candy-apple red Mustang—slanted next to my beat-up Accord. There's a trail of dust hovering above the dirt road leading to my house. No way my neighbors won't recognize it as hers. There are plenty of Mustangs in town, but hers is the only one with a FRONT STREET BAPTIST CHOIR bumper sticker on one side and THE PTA GETS THINGS DONE on the other.

She grabs my lapels and kisses me hard. I would have liked it better if she'd been kissing me like she meant it rather than pouring off anger about whatever brought her to my door. I ease back a tad, teasing the edge of her lips with my tongue. This woman is melted-sugar hot and the taste of her makes me weak. I still don't know why she arrived at my door in the middle of the day for God and all creation to see, and I'm starting to care less and less.

By the time she releases me, I'd let her add a bumper sticker declaring I'M FUCKING KC HILL.

"I'm going to kill that bastard." Lonnie's eyes are on fire, and not the good kind of fire that says I've touched her in just the right way. Nope, this is more of a spitting-mad kind of fire.

I step away. No way I want to get caught at ground zero if she decides to give life to that temper of hers. Fortunately, Southern women are simple—a glass of whiskey and a little bit of time is the standard therapy session. I pour four fingers of Jack Daniels, add some ice and pass it to Lonnie.

"Thanks, sugar." She closes her eyes and tips the glass. The lines of her face soften.

I wait until the first sip passes her lips and ask, "Which bastard?" No doubt she's talking about her husband, but since I like to pretend he doesn't exist, I force her to tell me.

She drains the whiskey and hands me the glass before answering. "That no-good, lying, cheating man I married."

I debate refilling the glass. If Glen cheated on Lonnie...mercy. She'll need more comfort than I—and an entire fifth of JD—can offer her. I set the glass on the counter.

The flush in Lonnie's cheeks runs down her neck and covers her chest. Explosion be damned, I want to touch, to ride the wave of her slightly labored breathing with my tongue. I move closer to her, bend my face to her neck and inhale deeply. The sweet subtle scent of honeysuckle and lavender surround me, drawing me in. I exhale long and soft against her skin. "Tell me what happened."

She tilts her head to the side, opening the line of her neck to me. "Glen's having an affair."

"I'm sorry, baby." I trace my fingers over the buttons closing the front of her dress and sprinkle whisper kisses across her chest, following the line of her open collar to tease the hint of cleavage.

"With a woman half his age, no less." Her words are softer, less combative.

"Really?" I press in tighter, drawing her to me. That Glen would have an affair with a younger woman doesn't surprise me. That it would be a condemning point for Lonnie does. I run one hand down her side, over her hips, lower and lower as I inch the fabric of her skirt up with my fingers.

"She's younger than Leann." Lonnie stiffens slightly and I circle her with my other arm, spreading my fingers wide against her low back and holding her firm against me. Leann is Lonnie's youngest daughter. At twenty-three, she's a year older than me.

"Mmm." There's not much else I can say. It's not like I can point out the irony of her last statement. That'd bring a halt to my hand gliding up her stocking-covered thigh right quick. I reach the lace edge of the stocking and trace the line between skin and nylon, barely touching with the tips of my fingers. Normally I'd take the time, drop to my knees, roll them to the floor. I love her legs, love to reveal them inch by inch. Today I want her to stop thinking about Glen and focus on me.

"I walked in on them in his office." Lonnie inhales sharply when my fingers make their way to the apex, ghosting over the satin fabric of her panties. I tease it to the side, brushing my index finger over the short curls and soft skin. "His goddamn office, KC."

I push one finger slowly inside her and she gasps. She's used to more foreplay from me. I'll gladly spend hours kissing every inch of her body, deliriously happy to feel her heat seep into me. She may be surprised by my approach—she's still dressed and standing in my entryway—but she's definitely ready. She shifts slightly, opening herself up to me, and her arousal, hot and wet, slides down my finger and coats my hand.

"Everyone knows." She half whispers, half moans, and I'm given the answer to why she parked in front of my house in the middle of the day. I'm no longer her dirty little secret; now I'm her revenge fuck. I slide out and push back in, quick and hard, two fingers this time, and she whimpers.

I maneuver her back, shuffling with my fingers still inside her, curling and uncurling, teasing her G-spot as we go—left foot, curl; right foot, uncurl—until her back is against the wall and I'm pressed tight against her. Her breathing is erratic and hot against my face. I hold my lips just out of her reach, content to share her air as I pump into her.

Her eyes slip shut and her head falls back against the wall. "I'm filing for divorce."

I fuck her harder, grasping her leg just below the knee and drawing it up to my waist. I use my hips for extra power. I want her to feel me tomorrow, long after she's gone home to him. I can feel her drawing tighter and when she comes I want to be the only person on her mind. "Next time call on your way over." I speak against her mouth, still not kissing her, but close enough to tease her lips with my tongue. "And I'll wear my strap-on."

"Yes." She gasps and digs her fingers into my shoulder. She's got long, manicured acrylics and even through the fabric of my shirt, I know she'll leave a mark.

"I'll bend you over the back of my sofa and fuck you from behind." I generally avoid vulgarities with Lonnie. She's precious, like china, and I like to fill her slowly and watch as she overflows. But today she needs to be taken in a way that makes her forget about her husband and his lover who is half her age. I move my mouth to her ear. "That would be so fucking hot. Your panties around your ankles, skirt around your waist, and your ass rocking back to meet my cock." I suck hard on her pulse point, forgetting that she always cautions against leaving marks.

Lonnie grips my head to her throat and thrashes her hips against mine. She's satin smooth and heaven soft around me, and I don't want it to end. I can feel her getting closer, her muscles drawing tighter. Her legs begin to shake as I smooth my palm over her hip and around to squeeze her ass.

"Oh, my god. Don't stop." She grinds her teeth together, catching my shoulder between them. "Don't you dare fucking stop." Lonnie is a loud, appreciative lover, a shouter, a moaner. Today her words are strangled, like she's choking back the moment.

"Let it go, baby." I add a third finger and she groans, her hips thrusting forward. She's tight and my fingers cramp together. Any mobility I had to twist and massage is gone. This isn't about finesse and gentle caressing, it's about power and pushing deeper and harder and faster.

One final push and she collapses in my arms, tears streaking down her face. She's quivering, that uncontrollable jerking that comes from being fucked properly, and her shoulders are shaking. I remove my hand as gently as possible and wrap my arms around her.

"Why'd he do it?" Her mascara runs, circling her eyes.

I lead her to the bedroom and sit her on my bed. "Wait right here." I press a soft kiss into her hair.

Perhaps another glass of whiskey, or a nice, hot, bubble bath? Bubbles rank right up there with Jack Daniels for problem-solving abilities. First things first. I get a warm washcloth and wipe the makeup from her face, whispering nonsense words as I go.

"I should leave him." She grips both my hands in hers, desperate and tight.

I nod. "You should."

"What would I do?" She's asking a question she knows the answer to. She doesn't need him. She's a Southern woman who aspires to Scarlett O'Hara greatness. No matter the adversity, she will overcome. That's just the way of things. But she looks so sad, so lost.

"You could stay here. With me." I say it casually with a shrug. She'll say no, and I should be happy that she came to me today. When she needed comfort, she chose me. Not her best friends at the country club, not her own daughters, and not the husband she leaves me for every other time we're together. She's always been so careful, has me trained so well to hide my feelings in public. The thought of her car parked in front of my house gives me a simultaneous wave of nausea and tingle of excitement.

She laughs, throaty and soft, and cups my cheek, her thumb smoothing back and forth over my skin. "Oh, sugar, you're so sweet."

"Not trying to be sweet." I open the buttons on the front of her dress slowly and slide it off her shoulders. "Who wouldn't want to wake up next to you every day?" I kiss along her jawline, down her neck, into the tight cleavage as I reach around and loosen the hooks on her bra.

"Your mama would kill me." My mama sings soprano to Lonnie's alto in the church choir; they went to school together, stood up for each other when they got married and babysat each other's kids when we were little. She's right. Mama would kill her.

"I'd kiss it better." I suck a nipple between my lips, grazing my teeth over the tip. The buckle holding her belt in place is stubborn. I move away from her slightly and focus on releasing it. More than anything, I want her naked and stretched out before me.

"Let me." She loosens the belt easily and stands. The fabric pools at her feet.

"You're beautiful." I brush my hands over her skin, palms flat, fingers spread wide. I want to touch all of her.

She shifts her weight from her left to right foot, then steps out of her heels. Garter belt, sheer black stockings and satin panties, and I'm panting at the sight of her. With past lovers I would rush, bent on getting to the prize. With her, there's too much pleasure in unwrapping the layers to hurry through.

"What are you doing with me?" This is a variation on a question she asks almost every time we are together. Usually it's the other way around; she wants to know what *she's* doing with me.

I kneel before her, working steadily to unfasten the clasps holding her stockings in place: first the front on her right leg, followed by a kiss to the exposed skin, then the back on the same leg. I want to kiss there as well, but it would involve too much maneuvering. She's uncertain right now and I need to keep her grounded in the moment with me. Instead of using my lips, I caress the flesh of her thigh, teasing upward to finger the edge of her panties. A shiver runs through her and I kiss her again, this time a little closer to center.

"Let's get this other one off, too." I speak softly. I want my words to be just as seductive, just as comforting, as my touch.

With both sides unhooked, I carefully, slowly roll the stockings down her legs. I love this process, the gradual revealing of her skin. It's like opening the best Christmas present ever. When I reach her feet, she steps out of the stockings. I fold them in half and place them on top of her shoes. She's almost naked and we're both shaking. I debate letting her lie down, but I don't want to do that until she's stripped bare.

I run both hands up her legs, gliding over her skin, but not really touching. I stop when I reach her panties, fingering the very edge but not letting myself go farther. I want them off so much that I don't trust myself not to fumble.

"Take..." My voice is too rough. I swallow and try again. "Take these off for me?"

She doesn't take nearly the care that I did with her dress and stockings. Rather, she pushes them down, garter belt and all, hastily, breathing hard and kissing me in an awkward, crunched-over-in-the-middle position that is sexy in its desperation. When she pulls out of the kiss, I chase after her with my lips, mouth partly open. She leaves me dazed.

Lonnie's had twenty-five years longer than me to learn the art of seduction, and she's a master. She lies on the bed with her elbows, chest jutting out. "I want to feel you."

She doesn't ask for this often, preferring, I think, not to be reminded of the show of age on her body. Before she can change her mind, I strip—in a very unsexy manner—and trip onto the bed, my jeans caught around my ankles. I curse, remove my boots and push my pants off. Lonnie laughs.

"What you lack in style, you definitely make up for with enthusiasm."

I crawl up her body, holding myself over her, close enough to feel the electric connection but too far to touch. This is a recurring theme with our lovemaking, the barely there caress. She's so far above me, she feels out of reach. No matter how many times she comes with my name on her lips, I can't believe she's here with me. If I touch her wrong, grip her too hard, she might disappear completely.

Rather than settle on top of her, I curl into her side. Even this limited contact with her is overwhelming. I drag my fingers down her side in a lazy pattern. I want to take her again, but she deserves to be cherished, savored thoroughly.

"You didn't answer my question." She wraps her arms around me, solid and tight.

"Which question?" I can't focus when we are this close. My world is narrowed to the throbbing pulse between my legs and the answering hum I feel from her body.

"Why are you with me?" She holds my gaze, and her chin wavers slightly. I hate that Glen's indiscretion is making her question herself.

"Because I'm lucky." I press a small kiss to her throat and spread my palm over her tummy, covering the network of stretch marks across her abdomen. I focus on one and trace it until it fades and a new one starts close to it.

She places her hand over mine. "How can you say that? Those lines are older than you." Her oldest was four years ahead of me in school.

"Those lines are beautiful." I kiss her belly, soft little butterfly kisses touching as many as possible. I love the parts of her body that she sees as imperfection. The way her breasts rest heavy and low. The web of stretch marks traveling toward her pubic area. The swell of her hips, generous and lush. All of these tell of her life. She's a story to be read and enjoyed often. "So sexy."

When she arrived, she needed to be possessed, taken. With that urgency sated, she lays her emotional insecurities out for me to hold tenderly until they don't haunt her quite so loudly. I hope to god I'm worthy of such trust.

She runs her hands through my hair. It's long and full of tangles, and I think fleetingly of cutting it short. A cute little spiky butch cut. I mentioned it to Lonnie once, asked if she liked it.

She looked stricken. "If you do that, KC, everyone will *know*."
Funny that her closet is big enough to contain both of us.

"I believe it when you say it," Lonnie whispers and pulls
me up, face-to-face. The look in her eyes is deep and slightly
wounded, but also showing the knowledge that she will be
okay.

I kiss her, letting my tongue slip between her lips. Everything about her, about our relationship, passes between us in the
perfect, soft glide of her tongue against mine. "Believe it because
it's true."

I think she might touch me then, more that the fleeting brush
of her fingers through my hair, but she doesn't. Rather she pulls
me on top of her, the worry in her eyes replaced by lust and
determination.

"You mentioned a strap-on..." She blushes when she says it.
It's cute and sexy, like a shy schoolgirl determined to be bad.

"I did." I glide my hand down her body, touching more firmly
now, caressing the curve of her hip. "But right now I'd rather
just touch you." I slip my fingers between her legs, smoothing
her desire over her clit. I want so bad to slide down her body
and take her into my mouth, to drink every drop she has to offer.
More than that I want to look in her eyes, to stay right here with
her while I stroke her over the edge.

She spreads her legs and I straddle her thigh. We moan
together as I coat her skin with my arousal. If I'm careful and
focus on anything but the sexy woman beneath me, I might just
be able to hold off my own orgasm until she's ready to come
again. I love coming with her. Just the thought sends a bolt of
desire through me.

I circle her clit, slow and easy, just saying *Hello, good to see
you again.* Maybe in a few minutes, after she's come and come
down, I'll slip on my strap-on and fuck her hard again. We've

never done that. I'm surprised she asked so boldly. That kind of initiative deserves reward.

For now, though, I'm lost in the slip-glide of my fingers over her sex, the roll of her hips as she thrusts up to meet me. Her muscles quiver, she's so close again, and I can give in to the rising pulse of need inside me. No need to hold back with her. She's always so hot, so ready, when she comes to me—insatiable. Yet she wants to know why I'm with her. How could I not be?

I tease her opening, just the hint of slipping my fingers inside and she holds perfectly still, her body coiled tight. I could push into her and push her completely beyond reason. Instead I hold my fingers there, thrashing my pussy against her thigh, the friction bringing me higher. The movement drives me farther into her, cupping her clit with my palm, my full weight behind it. She writhes against me.

The world is reduced to the hot pull of her body beneath me, and I can't hold out a moment longer. I thrust my fingers inside of her, and she cries out. "God, yes." She clutches my wrist, forcing me out, then back in again, harder than before. She's bucking against me, demanding I meet her rhythm. Lord knows I want to. She is wild, her body tight as she jerks her hips. And then she pulls tight, her eyes squeezed shut, head thrown back, and she releases a warrior's cry, a long, drawn-out, "Yeeeesssss."

There is nothing sexier than Lonnie when she lets go. One last thrust against her leg and I'm spent. I forget to hold myself off her, laying my body over hers, panting and head spinning.

I'm desperate to make sense of her visit to me, but I know I won't be able to. When I sit back, evaluating if she wants more or if she's done with me for now, she smiles, all honey and molasses.

"Sugar, that's just what I needed." She pats my bottom and shifts beneath me. She's ready to go home and I'm in her way.

I watch as she dresses, not bothering with my own clothes. A shower is in order. She pauses at the door and looks back at me over her shoulder. "I'll call before I come over next time."

As the door sweeps shut behind her, my short-lived fantasy that she might open her life to me is shattered. She's on her way home to her husband, and she'll probably scream and yell and throw things. Ultimately, however, she'll forgive him. With the click of the door latching, I'm once again reduced to the status of dirty little secret.

ARE YOU GONNA BE MY GIRL?

Jade Melisande

It's late afternoon. Ahead of us the sun is beginning to set, dull gold and orange streaking the undersides of clouds where the sky meets the road. Keri sleeps on the bench seat next to me, her head on my shoulder, her breathing a soft counterpoint to the mellow jazz I have on the radio. We've been traveling this way, her dozing, me driving, for about six hours.

"Keri," I say, "I got to stop for gas. You need to go to the bathroom or want something to snack on?"

She stirs drowsily, blinking, realizes where her head has been for the last two hours and straightens self-consciously. She stares muzzily out the window. We are twenty-five miles from nowhere, the road snaking through verdant fields of tall corn on either side of us. "Where are we?" she asks.

What she really wants to know is: how far have we gotten? Far enough?

"We've made it about three hundred and fifty miles," I say, answering her unspoken question. She turns eyes like dark bruises to me, searching my face briefly, before turning back to the window.

"Sign said there's a town five miles ahead. We can stop and get gas, stretch our legs. Give the Beast a rest." I pat the dash of the Chevy lovingly. The old girl's been a trouper, driving clear across the country with hardly a protest. They don't make them like they used to anymore.

"Sure," she says listlessly. I want to reach out to her, to pull her back over to me, but, hesitant for all kinds of reasons, I settle for touching her hand lightly.

She doesn't flinch or pull away.

"It'll be okay," I say.

She takes a breath, quick and shallow, doesn't reply.

I don't push it. *I* know she'll be okay. She just needs to know it—to believe it—too.

At the gas station she heads into the store for a soda while I fill the Beast with gas and check the fluid levels.

I am leaning against the truck as she comes out of the convenience store. I pretend that I am watching the gas pump, watching the numbers on the screen flash by, but really I am watching her, thinking about her, thinking about what I would do if she were mine to do things to. I can't help it; I have been thinking these thoughts for three hundred and fifty miles as she slept next to me, her round cheek pressed against my arm, her soft breasts rising and falling beneath her T-shirt like the road winding through the cornfields, easy, gentle.

I've been thinking of the last time I saw her, before this five-hundred-mile trek. The girl walking toward me now has the wary look of a hurt animal, so different from the ebullient, animated woman I watched walk out of my life a year ago. I've thought a lot about that last night with her, about feeling her lips on mine, the taste of wine on her mouth, her warm tongue slipping tentatively against mine, testing, tasting. I wonder if I'd taken advantage of what she offered that night, would we be here now; would she ever have left as she had, following her lover to Amarillo, and heartbreak?

I'd wanted her since I'd met her at a party the year before. We'd been friends right from the start, but friendships with straight girls can be precarious. You've got to be extra careful, be sure that you aren't stepping over any boundaries. Still, there were moments, glances, a smile, a touch of her hand. One night, after a concert in the park, we'd sat in the dark on our blanket after it was over, talking about men and relationships and our hopes and our dreams, sharing so much of ourselves that I thought maybe, maybe, this was it. I was tired of being careful, tired of exercising caution. I'd reached over to stroke her hair back from her face, then leaned over and touched my lips to hers, so gently, a question. For one heart-stopping moment she had kissed me back, her lips parted, her mouth soft against mine.

Then, abruptly, she'd pulled away. "I'm not ready for this, Laura," she'd said.

I'd turned away, looking into the warm, star-filled night and felt all my hopes balled up inside of me, a tight fist of disappointment. But I was her friend before anything else and wouldn't jeopardize that, no matter how much it hurt. And so I had stuffed down my desire and turned to her with a smile, easing the moment with some joke or other.

Life had gone on as before.

Until that night. We'd had too much wine, and her mouth was so sweet, her body so willing, pressed against mine in the doorway of my bedroom. My hands were aching to roam over her full breasts, longing to feel her nipples pucker against my palms, to taste her sweetness, to fill my nose and my mouth with the scent and taste of her.

I couldn't do it. I had held her for a long moment, breathing her in, wanting her with an ache that traced its way from my brain to the throbbing place between my legs, and then, reluctantly, pushed her gently away. I wanted her so badly...but not that way. Not with the wine blurring her senses. I wanted her to want me because she *wanted* me. So I'd put her in a cab and sent her home to her boyfriend-of-the-week, but her face, peering out the back window of the cab as it pulled away, had visited me in my dreams for weeks.

Six months later she was moving to Amarillo, Texas, with her latest boyfriend. And now here I am, picking up the pieces of that broken romance. What am I doing here?

I look over at her. As I watch, she pulls her hair up off her neck with one hand, allowing the capricious Kansas breeze to cool her. For the first time since I picked her up, I see the stress of the past year falling away. I see *his* shadow leaving her.

And I want her, suddenly, acutely, the desire flaring though me almost painfully in a flash of heat so bright I swear she must see it all the way across the parking lot.

If she were mine, I think, watching her, I'd call her over to where I am leaning against the truck. I'd reach out and pull her to me, sliding my hands from her hips to her waist, around her back; I'd pull her close, close enough to feel my heart hammering in my chest. She'd hesitate, resisting just a bit as I slid one hand up to the nape of her neck, under the thick fall of her dark hair. I'd hold her there, just like that, feeling her breasts press against mine, feeling their softness, their fullness, waiting to feel her yield to me. With my hand in her hair I'd pull her closer still and lean in to place my mouth just there, against the side of her throat. I'd taste the salt on her skin from the long day we've had, I'd smell the sweet girl scent of her, I'd feel the silky smoothness of her skin against my lips. I'd press my body all along hers and feel the shudder run through her as I bit her, so gently, my tongue barely touching her skin. I'd feel the quick breath she would take, feel the moment she yielded, pressing her hips closer to mine.

And the past year would blur behind us, unimportant, unreal.

She isn't mine though.

She reaches the truck and looks at me quizzically; I have been staring silently at her. Our eyes meet over the bed of the truck. I wonder what she sees in mine: Does she see the desire, the regret? Does she know how much I wish I could turn back the clock to that night, a year ago?

I drop my gaze. There are no do-overs in life.

She climbs silently into the truck beside me. I put the truck in gear and pull out, back onto the empty highway. Full dusk has fallen now, the clouds stained the same wine purple as her lips had been that night. The miles fall away behind us. She may not be mine, I think, but at least she is no longer his. Perhaps I am helping her find her way to being her own again.

I reach out to turn on the radio and feel movement next to me, then the soft touch of her hand on mine. "Laura," she says, so softly I can barely hear her over the hum of the engine.

I cut my eyes sideways at her. She is staring at me, her eyes wide and almost glowing in the half-light. "Pull over," she says. "Please, at the next crossroad."

I see a dirt track off to the right barely visible up ahead and dutifully pull off, watching the dust billow behind the truck as we pull through tall rows of summer corn. The corn is so high it waves above the roof of the truck, encircling us in a tunnel of green. She turns the door handle and steps out into the twilight to stand by the side of the truck, arms crossed over her chest. Confused and more than a little concerned, I push open my door and hop out too, then go around the front of the truck, trailing my hand along the hood and hearing the engine ping as I walk by.

"Keri? You okay?"

I stop in front of her, search her down-turned face. I want to reach out to her, but again, I hesitate, not sure where this mood has come from, or where it has taken her. Finally she looks up at me.

"Do you ever..." She pauses, swallows, starts again. "Do you ever think about that night, Laura?"

My breath catches in my throat. I don't pretend not to know what she's talking about. "All the time," I whisper. I'm not sure she'll hear me over the thunder of my heart. "I can't stop thinking about it."

I feel her yearning—and her hesitation. She remembers the last time, too, and my rejection of her.

"Keri..." I say. A breeze soughs through the cornstalks; they sway toward us, as if to enfold us in their green embrace. Her longing reaches tentative fingers across the pregnant space, seeking, drawing me near. Our eyes lock.

Now I'm the one who hesitates. Will I just be her next "lover-of-the-week"? In this moment it could go either way.

I let her go once; I won't do it again.

With a shuddering sigh I reach for her, pull her against me. She presses herself to me and my mouth is on hers and her lips are so soft, just as I have remembered, dreamt about, all this time. Her mouth opens to me and our tongues touch, softly, almost tentatively at first, then deeply, sliding together as we taste each other for the first time in a year. She is so damned sweet I want to drink her up, swallow her, all of her, her taste and scent and feel. We press closer as though we will melt into each other, pass into each other through our pores, through our skin, through our desire.

She slides her hands around my waist, and she is no longer hesitant in the slightest, she is ferocious, pulling me closer, her hands and mouth devouring me, touching me everywhere. Her mouth slides down my throat; she nips and licks, her tongue a sharp heat on my fevered skin.

"God, Laura," she sighs in my ear, "I've dreamt of this."

I cup her full breasts in my hands, kneading them, brushing my fingertips against the pucker of her nipples through her T-shirt. With a shock I realize she isn't wearing a bra, and further, that she must have removed it at the gas station. I groan and pull her T-shirt up to reveal large, dark nipples, puckered in the half-light. I lean forward and take first one, then the other in my mouth, biting, suckling, pulling on them with my lips and teeth, not even bothering to go slow, to be gentle. She gasps and leans back against the truck, giving me better access, her hands on my shoulders and her head thrown back.

Then my hands are on the button of her jeans.

I look up at her, come back to her sweet mouth, kiss her, hard, again.

"Tell me you want this, Keri," I say, my voice hoarse.

She stares back at me with glazed, liquid eyes.

"Tell me you want this for more than just right now," I say, knowing I am asking too much, too soon, but unable to help myself. The cornstalks seem to stop their swaying, their endless sighing in the wind, to listen.

Slowly she reaches a hand up and cups it around the back of my neck, pulls me to within a breath of her lips. "I wanna be your girl," she says, and kisses me. Her mouth this time is as tender as that first kiss we shared under the stars after the concert, but then her tongue is touching mine again and I pull it into my mouth, suckle it like I did her nipple only moments before. Her hands join mine where I struggle with the button on her jeans, helping me to undo them. She tugs them down over her full, lovely curves as I slide my hand inside the loosened waistband. She is wearing strangely chaste white cotton panties and I cup my hand over her pubic bone, just holding her for a moment, as I continue to kiss her, to explore her mouth with mine. She moans and pushes against my hand, and I feel her heat under my fingers, feel how wet she is right through the crotch of her panties. I slip my hand inside the waistband and down over the tight curls I find there and down further, to the delicious wet fold of her slit. She is soaked, and I slip a finger into her and then another when she spreads her legs and opens herself to me.

She tips her head back and closes her eyes, and I am watching her now, mesmerized, watching the way her throat works as I push my fingers in and out of her cunt, as I circle her clit with my thumb. She breathes raggedly and I fuck her in time to the motion of her hips as she pushes against my hand.

I can't take it anymore. I have to taste her. I consider laying her back on the seat of the Beast, but that would mean stopping what I am doing, and I can't do that. I drop to my knees in the dirt of the cornfield and pull her underwear over her hips. Her pussy is as beautiful as I had imagined it to be, all those nights, lying in my bed with only my own fingers for company.

I groan and push my face into her, simply breathing in her clean, pungent scent, the smell of her arousal, of her heat. As I press my mouth to her lips she gasps, and then, when I pull her clit into my mouth, gently sucking, she sighs and opens herself up farther to me. I slide my tongue along her opening and then plunge it inside, alternately lapping at her and fucking her with my tongue, aware of every sound she makes, every sigh, every movement.

She wraps one leg around my neck, pushes her fingers into my hair. I return to her clit and begin to suck and stroke it with more determination. She moans and grinds her cunt into my face, thrusting, pushing into my mouth. "Please," she says, panting, "please…"

She is shuddering, trembling all over as the orgasm begins to wash over her. I plunge two fingers deeply inside her, thrust them in and out of her in time to my mouth as it builds, and finally, with a kind of keening wail, it crashes over her. I feel her clench around my fingers, taste her sweetness on my tongue. As the spasms subside, the sounds of the cornfield and an occasional car going by on the highway begin to make themselves known again.

I stand and wrap myself around her. Softly, I kiss her, feeling her smiling against my mouth.

"Come on," I say, helping her with her clothing. "Let's go home."

DANGER

Sacchi Green

Sex. Anonymous, no-strings, cunt-clenching, blast-furnace sex, enough to get me through a few more months of repression: that's all I was looking for. But deep down, it wasn't that simple. What I needed was danger, or pain, or pleasure: anything intense enough to fill the void.

Cruising Greenwich Village wouldn't block out flashbacks to Vietnam, not a chance. But the war had cursed plenty of us with more than nightmares and memory lapses and the whole PTSD bag. Only somebody who'd been there could understand the addiction, the need for adrenaline highs. Sometimes sex was the closest you could come. If you got really, really lucky, it might even make you forget for a while.

After a year at a field hospital in the boonies at Pleiku and six months at the main facility in Long Binh, I'd finally been rotated "home" and assigned to an Army orthopedic ward. It didn't feel like home. I didn't fit stateside anymore, didn't fit anywhere, and over there the war still ground on into a future I wanted no part of.

There wasn't much of anything I did want, except enough of what passed for sanity to get me through my days. But I was needed; broken men who deserved far more depended on my care, and to keep from flaming out at my job I had to get away from it, if only briefly. So, on a rare weekend off, I took the train from DC to New York, and then the subway, rolling into the Christopher Street station at half-past midnight on June 28, 1969.

Sweat, piss and pot smoke soured the underground air. The street-level atmosphere was more breathable, but with an electric edge to it, a manic energy driving the crowds. I wasn't the only one looking for trouble. Local talent and weekend wannabes, hippies, hustlers, aging beatniks, tourists sucking up the scene wound in and out of bars and side streets along Sheridan Square. There were mostly guys, but a few women of interest caught my attention as I edged through the throng.

The fringe on a leather jacket brushed my arm in the cross-walk. A sideways glance showed me a lean, tanned face framed by black hair, small feathers tucked into each long braid. I felt a swift jolt of attraction—but my interest would fizzle if the body beneath the Indian regalia turned out to be male. I couldn't make up my mind until I'd dropped back far enough to watch her hips and long legs. I could make out a nice ass under the worn jeans, slim, but definitely female. Hippie role-play getups usually leave me cold; on the other hand, a nice touch of sexual ambiguity heats me up, so she'd scored at least a draw.

Once on the sidewalk, she turned and eyed me with more than the usual speculation, as if she thought she'd met me somewhere or was considering trying that line of approach.

I needed some decompression time. My gaze drifted past hers with only the subtlest pause at her slim, strong hands, as brown as her face. Maybe we'd connect later, if she turned up at one of the bars I'd be checking out. I kept on toward my friend's apartment just off the Square on Grove Street and felt the stranger watching me, felt my own stride alter subtly. My ass tingled. Then I heard her boots on the pavement as she moved away in another direction.

The leather-fetish shop just up the way was closed, but I took a look into its brightly lit windows anyway, reinforcing the sense that no, Dorothy, we weren't in Kansas anymore, thank you very much. Or in Washington DC at Walter Reed Army Hospital, although some of the S/M gear with its metal rivets and buckles gave me an unsettling flashback to the orthopedic ward.

I shook it off. Something different niggled at my mind as I dug out my keys and let myself in through the outer door. Kansas, Dorothy...a headline glimpsed at the newsstand in Penn Station... Oh, right. Judy Garland's funeral had been today. Maybe that explained the crowd's tension, maybe not. I hadn't been a huge fan, but still... I paused for breath on the fourth floor landing and murmured sincerely, "Thank you, Dorothy, really, thank you very much." Then my key clicked in the old lock, and I went on in.

My college friend, off in Kenya now with the Peace Corps, still hung on to her rent-controlled apartment. I chipped in for occasional weekends. The anonymity of the city suited me, and the edginess of the Village. Not to mention the potential for sex, with all its dangers. Okay, especially with all its dangers.

By ten past one I was showered and ready to roll. Jeans and a denim vest over a gray T-shirt, auburn hair just brushing my earlobes. Not advertising, exactly, but not discouraging anybody who might be shopping.

Sheridan Square was boy-bar territory. I took a look around, though, the memory of the tall stranger percolating to the surface of my mind. The notion of slipping my hands under that fringed suede jacket took on considerable appeal. The thought of her fingers under my own shirt roused my nipples to parade-ground attention. Had I missed my chance?

The crowd was even edgier now. Some folks went about business as usual, whether strutting or furtive, while others clustered in muttering groups. I paused outside the Stonewall Inn. The usual go-go boys didn't interest me, although some of the drag queens could be as much fun to watch as high femmes, when I was in the mood.

But flashy drama wasn't on my wish list tonight. I needed the touch of smooth, unscarred skin, the press of an unbroken body needing no more healing from me than the frenzy of mutual friction could provide. I needed a woman.

No drama? So what the hell am I doing on the streets of Greenwich Village after midnight?

And there it came, like the answer to a subconscious prayer. Four black-and-whites and a paddy wagon squealed to a halt in front of the Stonewall Inn. Cops poured out like circus clowns, rushing to get an eyeful in the bar before the "degenerates" slipped out the back.

It was a regular routine: a flurry of arrests, a few fleeing customers who couldn't afford to be outed, some stiff fines and then business as usual by the next night. But this time was different, and if you travel in the circles I do, or even if you don't, there's no need to explain the difference. Stonewall is in the history books.

My first instinct was to back off and head for more likely hunting grounds. Other folks seemed to have the same reaction, and the square was emptying fast. I walked a few blocks, going with the flow. But then the sirens of police reinforcements tore through the heavy air and instead of accelerating our retreat, turned the tide. Why did they need reinforcements? Something was happening. Something we didn't want to miss.

Back in the square screams and shouts and the crash of breaking furniture came from the Inn. A tangle of cops with billy clubs and drag queens wielding lethal spiked heels came flailing out onto the sidewalk. The queers were fighting back!

And so, suddenly, was the crowd, scream by scream, stone by stone, chaos racing on a torrent of long-repressed rage.

I was near the front, with no thought but to ride the wave of excitement, until I saw her thirty feet away. Dark braids flailed like whips as four cops tried to drag her toward the paddy wagon. I stared, caught her eye, and for an instant she flashed me a cocky grin, the fire of battle flaring in her eyes. She wrenched one arm free long enough to give me a thumbs-up sign. That brief glimpse of her hand hit me where it counted.

I swerved on impulse to charge to her aid, but a bottle shot past me from behind and exploded against a wall. War-zone reflexes slammed me to the pavement. When the crowd closed in it was move or be trampled, so I struggled upright and moved. By then there was no sign of her, and the cops were crouching behind their vehicle.

For an hour or so I hung around on the periphery of the action, not quite feeling like I had a right to be in the front lines. I'd never been hassled by the law, and in the military I'd kept a low, clean profile because my nursing was needed. Or so I told myself. Now I played medic to a few victims of shattered glass and pavement abrasions, applying disinfectants and Band-Aids from an all-night drugstore and ice packs rigged up in nearby bars. In between I cheered on the drag queens and pretty boys who turned the tables on the cops until the boys in blue had to barricade themselves inside the Stonewall Inn and call for more reinforcements.

Once in a while I caught distant glimpses of long black braids and a fringed jacket in the heart of the fight, where uprooted parking meters and benches were being used as battering rams to try to get at the police pinned down inside the tavern. She'd got loose, of course. Whenever I tried to get closer she disappeared into the shifting masses.

Frustration gnawed at me. All geared up, and nowhere to go: I'd come looking for sex, and the charged, manic atmosphere just pumped up my need, but this time groping in a secluded booth at a girls' bar wasn't going to do it for me. Even a wrestling match in a grubby restroom would be too tame. Even...

"Hey, medic, over here."

She was down a blind alleyway, slouching against a wall just at the blurred border where dim light gave way to darkness. Her fringed jacket was off, and slung over one shoulder.

Medic. She must have seen me patching up the wounded, but I hoped she wanted something more than first aid. Either way, I didn't hesitate for an instant. "Are you okay?" I didn't see any obvious signs of injury even when my vest brushed against her sweat-streaked tank top. "What do you need?"

No smile now, just a long, searching look into my eyes. My breathing quickened. So did my pulse rate, and an aching knot of need tightened my groin.

"What do *you* need, medic?" It wasn't a question. Her voice was low, husky and certain. My answer was a half step forward that brought me up firmly against her. One thigh pressed into her crotch, I straddled her slightly raised knee. Just a little more pressure, the slowest of movements...and the need was building, along with the haunting fear of giving in to a need for more than I could get.

A glare of blue light flashed past the end of the alley as a cop car sped by. My back was exposed, vulnerable. What if I were caught, arrested, disgraced, discharged...

The prickle of fear down my spine made my pulse beat even faster, my body strain harder to feel the responding pressure of hers. I clutched at her back, my hands already under her thin shirt, raising it. Her arms were around me, and she gripped my ass, forcing me to move, to rub against her in a rhythm that demanded fierce acceleration. "What do you need, what do you need," she muttered over and over, a low, compelling chant, and all I could do was move faster, rub harder, feel her hardened nipples flick across my aching breasts and slide my cunt along her thigh while my own thigh met her thrusts.

There were distant crashes...panic was threatening to take hold...but she edged a hand inside my jeans and wrenched all my awareness back to where our bodies merged. Her fingers slid through my folds into my hungry cunt, her thumb went at my clit with hard, sure strokes—and I plummeted over the edge, all defenses gone, all trust given, nothing mattering but to get more and more, harder, please, more!—until the whole battery of sensations, fear, urgent need, loss of control, came together in one massive jolt of pleasure.

It took a while to breathe again without panting. I knew I'd been dangerously noisy and didn't care. She still held me close, without demand, although I could feel her heavy breathing.

It was my turn to chant, "What do you need, what do you need..." but my voice was muffled, first against her sweaty throat, then in the swell of her high breasts, then in the curve of waist and belly and lower still. She was the one getting noisy now. By the time my knees ground into the alley's grit I had her zipper open and her briefs worked down enough to give my tongue and fingers access.

The intensity of her taste; the deep, rasping moans vibrating right through into my mouth; the flailing of long hair as her head thrashed back and forth—I wanted to savor all these, but I let the thrusting of her pelvis set the pace. The faster I licked and rubbed, the harder she needed it, until she came in such a flurry of violent jerks that I had to hold tight to stay with her. I managed to hang on, not easing up, until at last she pulled back and sank down beside me.

"So," she said between shuddering gasps, "you come here often, medic?"

"Never did an alley before," I said. "Always bars."

"And always strangers?"

"Always." I was still in too much of a post-fuck daze to think clearly.

She was quiet for a minute or two, catching her breath, maybe pondering in ways I was too dense to notice then. Finally she stood, giving me a hand to help me up. "All right then. Glad I qualified. Thanks for the ride. Maybe I'll see you around." She moved out of the alley into the light of the city, and then she was gone, leaving me with a hazy feeling that however well I'd been fucked, I'd somehow really fucked up.

The action in the alley had drained me, but only for a while. The turmoil of protest was still roiling up and down one street or another, recharging me to a high pitch of nervous energy, so I went to check out the girl bars after all. But I found no prospects that came close to what I needed, not that I even knew what I needed anymore.

When massive police forces with riot shields finally arrived, the battling crowds fragmented into pockets of guerrilla action and then drifted away like tendrils of pot smoke. Anybody left on the streets was in danger of arrest or worse. A remnant of survival instinct sent me hurrying back to the apartment.

"Hey...medic..." The voice was low this time, strained.

She emerged from the shadows across the street, exhausted, bedraggled, shivering, coming down from the high of surging adrenaline. The hair straggling loose from one braid was sticky with blood. "Come on in," I said, and unlocked the door.

After three flights of stairs, her face looked greenish in the harsh light of the kitchen. "Sit down," I ordered. "Head between your knees." She obeyed without question, long, strong hands braced on her booted ankles. I thought wryly that having her head between my own knees would have been my first choice in other circumstances.

She'd caught a hit above her left ear hard enough to split the skin and raise a still-swelling lump. "Did you pass out when you got hit?" I was cleaning the wound gently with a soaking wet dishtowel. I'd already had a look at her eyes and didn't see any signs of concussion.

"Nope. Just got real mad. And maybe a tad destructive." Her voice was getting steadier.

"You're lucky to have such a thick skull." I felt around through her hair for more damage.

"Lucky to find a cute nurse close at hand." A cocky attitude isn't easy to pull off with your head down and bloody water trickling over your neck and down your chin but she managed. There was something about the tone of voice and an old, raised scar across the nape of her neck that diverted the flow of reddened water... I knew with sudden certainty that "Haven't we met somewhere?" wouldn't have been just a hackneyed pickup line, after all. That scar was just about a year and a half old, the result of a mortar attack that blasted her ambulance apart and killed an already-wounded soldier. Her collarbone had been broken, too, but she'd managed to get the other two guys out and away before flames hit the gas tank.

I let her sit up while I went to fix an ice pack. "What makes you think I'm a nurse?" That had been a stupid question—so much for anonymity. Not that she'd be likely to give me away to the Army bureaucracy, but some fear even deeper made my gut tense, some danger I couldn't even give a name.

"Well, you were one hell of a nurse in Long Binh, and I figure that's something you never forget. Like riding a bike. Or a woman." Her grin, now that I could see it, was cocky, too, but her eyes were grimly sober. She knew all about the things I couldn't forget. She'd been there, too, right through the worst of it. Her hair had been much shorter, not quite as dark, and the only time I'd seen her up close was when I was stitching up that gash on the nape of her neck. I might not have recognized anything about her, even my own handiwork—but I did remember the cockiness under stress. And those hands.

"You were in 'Nam, right? Ambulance driver?" I pressed the ice pack against her wound. "Hold that." Her hand went up obediently.

"Jeep jockey, mostly, on loan to the nurses' motor pool from the WAC base at Long Binh. When things got hot, every vehicle had to double as an ambulance."

I drew a deep breath. "And nurses had to be doctors half the time."

"Right." She held out the hand that wasn't holding the ice. "Thanks for the fine stitching job, Kim. I asked around about your name."

"You're more than welcome...Gale, isn't it?" I shook her hand, then forced myself to let it go. "Once we get the swelling under control, I'll put on a dressing, and you can hang out here tonight and get some rest."

Whether she had a concussion or not—could be a mild Class A—she had to be badly shaken, her defenses down. Better stick to the nurse role. "How about a bite to eat?" I went to the cupboard and riffled through it. "Hungry?"

"Could work up an appetite." Gale's tone made me glance back over my shoulder. She was surveying my ass and back with open appreciation.

"Definitely a sign of recovery." I put some chicken noodle soup on to heat. She didn't have such weak defenses, after all, if her offensive game was anything to go by.

"A little something to keep your strength up," I told her, once I'd set out soup and crackers for us both and sat down at the table to join her. Then, while she was still formulating a snappy comeback, I turned seriously apologetic. "I'm sorry I didn't recognize you sooner. It was...hard, over there, keeping a balance between caring enough about patients and not caring too much. And afterward there was so much to block out..."

She started to shake her head, and winced. "No problem. I figure I got more mileage tonight out of being a stranger." The grin she managed was strained. My various sensitized pulse points stirred hopefully at the reminder, but I swung back into nurse mode with an effort, gathering up disinfectant and scissors and bandages from the bathroom.

"Yeah, well..." I felt my face flush. "Back to business for now. This will sting a little. And I'm going to have to snip some hair around the wound site."

"Hack it all off," Gale said curtly. "If I hit the streets tomorrow looking anything like I did tonight, I'll be painting a bright red target on my ass. The cops are probably throwing darts at sketches of me right now. "

I gave her a trim that, bandage aside, left her looking like the teenaged love child of Katharine Hepburn and Marlon Brando: elegant cheekbones; short, unruly hair; sultry eyes. "You clean up pretty well," I told her. "The image of a target on your ass is pretty intriguing, though. You sure there isn't one there

already? Was all that" —I motioned toward the fringed jacket
and the braided, dyed hair showing above the rim of the wicker
wastebasket—"some kind of disguise? You're not just worried
about the local cops, are you?"

An attempted shrug made her wince again. She yawned and
rubbed her eyes, shock and exhaustion beginning to catch up to
her, but she answered me frankly. "I'm AWOL, and wanted by
everybody from the MPs to the Oakland Police Department to
the SDS. A little episode coming out of the Oakland Army Base
just after I got stateside."

I knew all too well the treatment a uniform could get you
back in the land of your birth. Even nurses ran the risk of
taunts and spitting when protesters got their mob mentality
on. I might agree with some of what they were for, but their
methods seemed like the mindless tantrums of overprivileged
brats. "That bad, huh?" I wished I hadn't brought up the
subject. She didn't need any more stress tonight.

"It wasn't what they yelled at *me*. I hadn't slept for forty-
eight hours, had waking nightmares, barely remembered my
own name, and I still kept my shit together through all that. But
there was this guy in a wheelchair, a Marine. When they threw
things, he couldn't get out of the way fast enough. I don't even
remember much after that, but I know I grabbed a *babykiller*
sign and started swinging it. Some people got hurt. I ran and
kept on running."

Her head slumped. I caught it against my breast as my
arms went around her. "Come on to bed now," I said, my lips
brushing her hair so lightly she couldn't have felt them. So
much for my longing for unscarred, unbroken women. What
a delusion.

She managed to stand, moved across to the bedroom with
my help and even tried to pull me down beside her while I eased

her clothes off. "Later," I said, and turned out the lights. "Get some sleep now. Nurse's orders."

A faint glow of sunrise already showed around the curtains. I sat and watched Gale sleep for a while, nearly dozing myself. I was wrung out and hyped up, a combination not optimal for clear thought.

A trash can lid clanged outside. A split second later an unearthly string of explosions rocked the air. Firecrackers, not grenades, I realized, after the first panicked lurch of my heart, but by then I was holding tight to Gale as she thrashed and kicked and yelled in short, incoherent bursts.

"It's all right," I said, soothingly and then more sharply, trying to penetrate her nightmare. "It's okay, all right, you're safe, I've got you." It took a while, and at least once her kicks knocked me off of the bed. "Cut it out!" I yelled at last, and then, as her eyes finally opened, I said, "It's me, Kim, the nurse, remember?"

She stared, still not quite awake. The kicking stopped, but shivering set in, in spite of the blankets I'd pulled over her. "It's all right," I repeated, pulling off my clothes. "You're safe, here, with me." I crawled under the covers to warm her and pressed my body along the length of hers. "Remember?"

"Medic," she muttered. "What...?"

"Just firecrackers in a trash can. It's okay. We're safe." I held her closer, and she relaxed a little. "Remember last night?"

Now her arms went around me. Relaxation gave way to something entirely different. "Remember last night? Always." She moved against me, sliding her body along mine, and I responded in ways wholly unrelated to nursing ethics.

"Careful," I said and rolled her gently on her back. "Don't move your head too much. Take it slowly, just let me... gently..." So she did, or tried, until the slow, achingly sweet movements of skin on skin, fingers stroking along curves and hollows and burrowing into deep warm places, mouths feasting on just about everything, led to rolling waves of pleasure that ultimately demanded a faster pace. Thrusts became harder, licks alternated with bites, until we were both sobbing in our desperate need—and then even harder in our release.

Gale slept again. I watched her face, vulnerable in this temporary illusion of safety, and faced my own vulnerability. Danger was a bond between us: the fear of it, the need of it, the inability to trust in peace. On some deep level, though, we did trust each other. That scared me right down to my bones. To open up, to let yourself care, was to offer a hostage to an ever-cruel fate.

She slept all day and then finally left as the protests were picking up steam again. "I have to move on, Kim. At least for now. Probably get into more trouble. I wish…"

"I know. I have to go back to work. People need me."

"I know all about needing you. If there are times—if I track you down…"

"I'll be there. No matter what, or when." I gave her an address that would always, eventually, reach me. And she did, many times over the years, when she needed healing, or bail money, or sex with nothing held back; until finally it wasn't necessary any longer. The time came when we needed to be together more than we needed danger, and by then there were places where the world had changed enough that we didn't have to hide from anything. Even ourselves.

ABOUT THE AUTHORS

CRYSTAL BARELA has been published in more than a dozen erotic anthologies.

JOVE BELLE (jovebelle.wordpress.com) lives in Portland, Oregon, with her partner of fifteen years and their three children. Her novels include *Chaps*, *Split the Aces* and *Edge of Darkness*.

CHEYENNE BLUE's (cheyenneblue.com) erotica has appeared in many anthologies, including *Best Women's Erotica*, *Lesbian Cowboys* and *Best Lesbian Romance*. She lives in Denver.

RACHEL KRAMER BUSSEL (rachelkramerbussel.com) has edited many books of erotica, including *Up All Night*, *Glamour Girls*, *First-Timers*, *Spanked*, *The Mile High Club* and the nonfiction collections *Best Sex Writing 2008, 2009* and *2010*.

ANDREA DALE's (cyvarwydd.com) stories have appeared in *Lesbian Cowboys*, *The Sweetest Kiss* and *Bottoms Up*, among many others. With coauthors, she has sold two novels to Virgin Books.

DEJAY's (dejaynovl.net) short stories can be found in *Khimairal Ink*, *Lesbian Cowboys*, *Year's Best Lesbian Fiction 2008* and *Nuance*.

DELILAH DEVLIN (DelilahDevlin.com) is an author with a rapidly expanding reputation for writing deliciously edgy stories with complex characters.

R. G. EMANUELLE is a writer and editor living in New York City. She is coeditor of *Skulls and Crossbones*, an anthology of female pirate stories, and her short stories can be found in *Best Lesbian Erotica 2010* and the 2010 issue of *Khimairal Ink*.

CATHERINE LUNDOFF is the author of *Crave: Tales of Lust, Love and Longing* and *Night's Kiss: Lesbian Erotica* and editor of *Haunted Hearths and Sapphic Shades: Lesbian Ghost Stories*.

SOMMER MARSDEN (SmutGirl.blogspot.com) is the workaholic, wine-crazed author of *Lucky 13*, *Corporeal* and *Bittersweet*, among other books. Her work has appeared in dozens of anthologies, numerous magazines and all over the web.

KENZIE MAYER works at a library in small town Alaska. Her passions are writing, painting, dogs, doughnuts, woods and ocean. This is her first published story.

JADE MELISANDE (piecesofjade.wordpress.com) is a sex blogger, polyamorist and published travel, erotica and fiction writer, as well as an all-around kinky girl.

REN PETERS has been published in the online anthology *Read These Lips, Volume 1* and in Bella's *Fantasy: Untrue Stories of Lesbian Passion*.

C. B. POTTS (cbpotts.livejournal.com) writes and edits incredibly boring stuff by day and sultry stories by night. You can find her stories in *Lipstick on Her Collar*, *Working Girls* and other anthologies, and follow the strange twists and turns of her life on her Live Journal.

TERESA NOELLE ROBERTS writes erotica that has appeared in *Bottoms Up*, *Dirty Girls*, *Best Women's Erotica 2004*, *2006* and *2007*, and many other anthologies with titles that make her mother blush. She also writes erotic romance for Samhain and Phaze.

MIEL ROSE's porn stories have appeared in *Best Women's Erotica 2008*, *Best Lesbian Erotica 2008*, *Best Lesbian Love Stories 2009* and *Ultimate Lesbian Erotica 2009*. You can find her personal essay on femme identity in *Visible: a Femmethology, Volume 1*.

FRAN WALKER (franwalker@ihug.co.nz) lives in beautiful Aotearoa/New Zealand. She is married to the fantasy novelist L-J Baker.

ABOUT THE EDITOR

SACCHI GREEN lives and writes in western Massachusetts. Her stories have appeared in numerous books, including seven volumes of *Best Lesbian Erotica*, four of *Best Women's Erotica*, *Best Lesbian Romance* and *Penthouse*. She has edited, or coedited with Rakelle Valencia, five previous lesbian erotica anthologies: *Rode Hard, Put Away Wet* (Suspect Thoughts Press); *Hard Road, Easy Riding* (Lethe Press); *Lipstick on Her Collar* (Pretty Things Press) and *Lesbian Cowboys* and *Girl Crazy*, both from Cleis Press.